| DATE | | |
|---|---|---|
| | | |

If you have a home computer with internet access you may:
   -request an item be placed on hold
   -renew an item that is overdue
   -view titles and due dates checked out on your card
   -view your own outstanding fines

To view your patron record from your home computer:
Click on the NSPL homepage:
http://nspl.suffolk.lib.ny.us

# Darwin's Nightmare

# Darwin's Nightmare

## MIKE KNOWLES

ECW Press

Published by ECW Press
2120 Queen Street East, Suite 200, Toronto, Ontario, Canada M4E 1E2
416.694.3348 / info@ecwpress.com

LIBRARY AND ARCHIVES CANADA CATALOGUING IN PUBLICATION

ISBN-13: 978-1-55022-842-7

Knowles, Mike
Darwin's nightmare / Mike Knowles.

I. Title.

PS8621.N67D37 2008          C813'.6          C2008-902383-8

Cover and Text Design: Tania Craan
Cover Image © Elisa Lazo de Valdez / Corbis
Typesetting: Mary Bowness
Production: Rachel Brooks
Printing: Friesens

This book is set in Sabon.

The publication of *Darwin's Nightmare* has been generously supported by the
Canada Council for the Arts which last year invested $20.1 million in writing and
pulishing throughout Canada, by the Ontario Arts Council, by the Government of
Ontario through Ontario Book Publishing Tax Credit, by the OMDC Book Fund,
an initiative of the Ontario Media Development Corporation, and by the
Government of Canada through the Book Publishing
Industry Development Program (BPIDP).

PRINTED AND BOUND IN CANADA

*For Andrea.*
*It could be for no one else.*

# CHAPTER ONE

Watching for the switch was the easiest part. This guy was such an amateur that he drew attention to himself just standing there. The bag, the object of my interest, was being held by a young kid with blond highlighted hair and several days' worth of dark scruff growing on his face. His small mouth was chewing gum, hard, and his head was looking around one hundred eighty degrees left then right. If he were capable he would have spun his head in a constant rotation, taking in everything in the airport. He couldn't even dress the part; he was wearing a long beige trench coat — unbuttoned with the collar turned up. The only thing missing was a fedora. I was sure he watched spy movies to pump himself up for the deal.

The deal itself was the only thing hard to figure. I had been paid to steal a package from an unknown person, and I had no knowledge about the courier, size, contents, or nature of the package. I knew only the location, Hamilton International Airport, which made any tools I wanted to bring pretty much useless. The airport was small in comparison to its counterpart, ninety minutes away in Toronto. The Hamilton airport ran about three hundred flights per week. Only one third of those flights were international. Most of the passengers who used the airport were businessmen on domestic flights to Ottawa or Montreal.

It was eight in the morning in mid-October, and the airport was in a lull. The passengers who had arrived on the red-eye had collected their luggage and gone outside, leaving only a hundred or so customers in the terminal. I had to intercept the bag before it got to a plane, and that meant I might have to follow it to a gate. So I came in light.

There were only a few minimum-wage rent-a-cops working as airport security near the entrance; there was no need for more. The crowds were sparse and half-asleep, and the real action took place after you bought your ticket. The blond kid moved around the terminal looking at brochures and the candy on display in the convenience store. I watched him and everything else in the terminal from a seat near a row of pay phones. No one else seemed to be watching the kid, which made me think the deal was going to happen on the other side of the metal detectors. Every so often, my gaze would catch the boy's blond hair, and I would focus on him. He was young, no more than twenty-five, and under the trench coat he wore a black Juventus soccer warm-up suit. The flashy labels on the casual clothes under the coat made the kid easy to spot. His light olive skin put his ancestors around the Mediterranean; the warm-up suit narrowed the geography to Italy. His hair had been dyed blond a few weeks ago, judging from the inch of dark roots visible above his forehead. He augmented his faux blond hair with a lot of gel, making him taller and more colourful than anyone around him. Everything about his outfit, his features, and the way he carried himself screamed, "Look at me!" He made no effort to be anonymous, to be invisible, like me. It made me wonder what I was doing involved with this kid, and it made me wonder about the bag. What could a kid like this be trying to move? And why would it be important to my employer?

Just when I thought it couldn't get any better, a watch started beeping. It was the kid's watch; the beeping startled him, and he shut it off so he could complete another full scan around the room. He moved toward a gate, and produced a ticket from an inner coat pocket. He would have to pass several small restaurants and stores to reach the double doors that led to the metal detectors. Only one of the doors was open, and there was a backup of ten or twelve passengers. I moved in behind the kid and took the roll of quarters from my pocket. If this guy was as amateur as he looked, it would all work out. I moved his coat to the side with my left hand and shoved the roll hard into his back right on top of his kidney.

"Turn around and walk to the bathroom *now*," I said, and shoved the roll of coins harder into his back like a gun barrel.

"What? . . . What are you doing? W . . . w . . . why?" he stuttered.

"Too bad, kid. If you didn't know, you would have screamed," I said into his ear. "Move out of line and walk to the bathroom. If you don't I'll just clip you here. The gun is silenced. I'll be in the car before anyone figures out you've been shot."

The kid didn't question me; he moved away from the line and turned toward the washroom as though he was being pulled by marionette strings. As we walked, the back collar of the beige coat became brown with sweat. The bathrooms were down a long hall, and we had to weave around several people to get to the door. If this poseur had been anyone else he would have shoved off and been mixed into the people before I could get any shots off. But he wasn't anyone else.

"Stop here," I said as we neared the handicap washroom. I pulled down an out-of-order sign I had taped to the door and ushered him in. I eased up on his kidney, and he made his move, just like I hoped he would. He pushed back, trying to trap me against the door, and spread his arms, ready to take the pistol. If I had a gun he might have taken it, though more than likely I would have put a bullet in him. My foot found the back of his knee, and his body shifted down until his knees hit the tiles on the floor. I drove my forearm across his jaw, hard, and heard the sound of it coming out of socket; his mouth must have been open. Both hands had risen up near his face when I palmed the roll of quarters and went to work on his back. Two hooks to each side of the kid's body put him flat on the floor gasping. I lifted the bag. It was light, lighter than I expected, almost as if it was empty. I got over my surprise and got back to the task at hand. It was time to go. I eased the blond kid back onto his feet and laid a tight uppercut into his jaw using the quarters.

# CHAPTER TWO

On the drive back to the office, there were no flashing lights in my rear-view, and no dark cars following in my wake. Even though I was sure that I had no tail, I manoeuvred the streets using random turns and sudden bursts of speed, keeping my eyes on the mirrors. No cars stayed behind my old Volvo, and no one on the street looked at the car twice. Its exterior was well worn, like most cars in the city, but I kept the guts in shape. The car was unobtrusive until it had to run; then you couldn't help but notice it — while it was still in view. The bag I had picked up was locked in the roomy trunk, unopened.

When I got to the office, I went right to the safe. I put the bag in and pulled out one of the ten prepaid cell phones that were arranged neatly inside. I closed the safe and took the phone over to the desk. The hard wooden chair groaned with my weight, but it held me without collapsing. I powered up the phone and dialled a number I had committed to memory.

"Yeah?"

"It's done," I said, and the line went dead. I knew from experience that I had an hour or two until pick-up — after that I could eat. I pulled my Glock 9 mm out of the top right desk drawer and set it in my lap, propped up against my thigh.

I waited, staring out the window, the chair leaned back and my feet resting on the windowsill so that I could see the street below. Across from my fifth-floor window was a worn-out high-rise, home to a number of small businesses like legal aid, a free clinic, and a blood donor centre. I spent an hour and ten minutes guessing which service each person entering would use. After ten minutes of inactivity on the building steps, I saw a woman in a fitted business suit make her way up the stairs. Each step bounced her large shiny purse off the back of her skirt. I imagined her at first to be a lawyer or doctor, but her bag was just a bit too shiny to be high-class. I pegged her for a working girl stopping into the clinic. Most of the working girls I knew tried to pinch every penny. No one wanted to work under men forever, and hookers needed condoms like offices needed paper clips. The sound of the door opening brought me back to reality. I swivelled in the chair, hand in my lap, to face the door.

"Morning, Julian. What's new?" Julian hated me and I knew it. I asked him questions because I knew it drove him nuts. He never had to answer questions to anyone but his boss, and I was certainly not him.

My pleasant, offensive good-morning was answered with a grunt as Julian moved toward the table. My hand instinctively tightened on the gun just as someone's hands would tighten on the wheel of a car if a bear walked toward the driver's side window. He was six foot four and at least three hundred pounds, but he didn't stomp; he glided to the desk and sat down. Julian was solid like a

12

MIKE KNOWLES

tree was solid, but he had some flab on his stomach and face. He wore grey cotton slacks and an untucked blue linen shirt. On the street people might think he was trying to be fashionable, but if you looked closely you would see that the shirt concealed an angular bulge at the base of his spine. The bulge was not a wallet; it was a gun, and judging by the size of the bulge, which I had seen on many occasions, it was big. The two of us enjoyed a friendly relationship; he showed up every once in a while and always left within five minutes. When he spoke he was pleasant, but under the pleasantries hid a killer. I had seen the real Julian once before, up close, and he had come out the winner. Julian had humble beginnings as a childhood friend and protector of Paolo Donati. He spent years looking out for the man who would one day be king of the streets. Julian was with Paolo for every step of his ascent. He went from being a leg breaker to working as the right hand of the most powerful mob boss in generations. He was the only person I saw when I worked for Paolo.

As Julian's ice-grey eyes stared into mine they momentarily lost their congeniality, but it returned as quickly as it had vanished. He was a pro, but there were some feelings he couldn't keep completely bottled up. His hatred slipped out like steam from a pipe ready to burst. He hated me and what I did, and he could never let that go. I stood, leaving the gun in the chair, and walked to the safe. I opened it and took the bag to the door. Julian rose without any indication of discomfort, placed a stack of bills on my desk, and moved to the door.

"What is it? In the bag, I mean. Did you look inside?" Julian always seemed unsure if anyone caught his meaning so he worked hard to make himself as clear as possible; he repeated himself over and over in different words, all meaning the same thing. It was an annoying habit, but I was sure no one told him that. I was also sure there would be a time when he wouldn't try to clarify his thoughts to me. When that happened, there would be trouble.

I opened the door, and he took the bag and walked out. He always asked the same question in some form or another. I never responded; I just held the door and let him walk. Julian knew I was a professional and that I hadn't looked in the bag. His question was a reminder that he beat me once, and that to him I was just an amateur. He used more syllables to say "fuck you" than anyone I knew.

After he was gone, I sat and watched the street again. I didn't see Julian leave — I never expected to — but I watched all the same. I thumbed through the money Julian had left on the desk; I didn't count it because I knew it would all be there. After a time I felt hungry.

I walked out the front door of the building, my own angular bulge in the back of my shirt. I walked down the street from the office, passing different windows that advertised sandwiches with more meat and less fat, some grilled, others toasted. I breezed past the advertisements until I came to a Vietnamese restaurant I frequented. The place was not a chain, and by no means a dive. The restaurant catered to Vietnamese people. Everyone who worked there and most of the people who dined there were from Vietnam. The menus were in Vietnamese with numbers and pictures for any interlopers who chose to stop in. The dining room smelled of spices and was heavy with steam from the kitchen. I took a seat in a corner of the dining room in a place where I could watch the street and the action inside. The lunch crowd was eating like it was Thanksgiving at the soup kitchen and no one looked my way — until a man stopped at the window.

He didn't slow and then stop; he stopped at the window, and put his face up to the glass. When his eyes found me, he was startled to see me looking back at him. He regained his composure, looked around for another ten seconds, then left in a hurry. I was surprised. It seemed the amateur from the airport had amateur friends who had identified and followed me. I ordered a number fifty-eight — the chicken soup, which was so much better than it sounded, and rice. I drank the cold tap water left for me out of a small glass half full of ice and contemplated how I had been followed to the office. No one had tailed me from the airport, so they had to know who I was. My thoughts were interrupted by the arrival of two steaming plates. The soup was a dark broth, and in the centre was a piece of chicken still on the bone. The rice was light brown and smelled heavily of green onions. I stared at the food and had more of my water. I knew that the food was far too hot and that I had to wait at least five minutes before I could even try to eat it.

After I paid the bill, I left the restaurant and walked three blocks up the street to the gym. The whole way there I used store windows to look around me, and made several trips across the street to see if anyone followed, but no one did. There were no scruffy kids in tan trench coats reading newspapers under lampposts or lurking in alleys.

The gym was like a time warp back twenty or thirty years. There were no treadmills or flashy machines; there was only iron, tons of it. No one manned the front desk, and there were no trainers in neon outfits spotting out-of-shape housewives and businessmen. The place was old-school and hard-core. Just inside the front door was a sign: "Train or leave." It wasn't the club motto, it was a command. If you weren't there to work, you weren't there at all.

I had a permanent locker at the gym, stocked with several pairs of pants, shorts, shirts, as well as a shaving kit, and a knife. I kept several places stocked like this because

I rarely went to the house I had spent my adolescence in, even though it was all mine and I was the only one living there. I showered at the gym and lived out of the office as much as possible.

I changed into old unwashed sweats, locked all my things in my locker, and made my way to the brightly lit workout floor. The room was well lit because it was a windowless box hidden deep in the concrete. It had a musty smell, like old shoes, which had developed over the past decade. There were only a handful of people there, not one of them talking over the loud thundering music. No one acknowledged my presence; they just kept on lifting. The majority of the people in the gym weren't large by body-building standards. The men here didn't lift to look good — they lifted for strength. These men were like ants. They easily moved twice their body weight with just arms and legs. I found a spot and got ready to dead lift. I spent half an hour moving weight off the floor to my waist and back down again. Once I finished, I moved the bar and weights around and devoted my time to the clean and jerk. The gym was full of cops, firemen, and people like me. All of us worked here to be better. There was an unspoken truce in the gym. Everyone knew what everybody else was outside the doors, but inside the walls of the gym it didn't matter. It wasn't uncommon for cops to spot career low-lifes while they pushed hundreds of pounds above their necks. Letting the weight fall would have saved blood, sweat, and countless hours of manpower, but no weights ever crushed anyone's throat. The gym was time off the battlefield. Time off that everyone was grateful for.

It had been more than a decade since I was first shoved in the door by my uncle. He dragged me to the gym and told me if I wanted to work in the adult world with him I had to be able to pull my own weight. No one would work on a job with a kid in his late teens who looked like a target for any bully wanting to kick sand in his face. Since that day, I had never stopped coming. I trained every day; it was that or go home to the empty house I hated so much.

After the workout I showered, staying long under the spray, letting the heat wash away the stiffness. Once I was back in my street clothes, I sat on the bench and began to consider my situation. I did a job and was paid. The only hang-up was that the owners of the bag had found me; that face in the restaurant window could only be a tail. I had a few options: I could lay low; I could call my employer; or I could handle it myself. I wasn't going to run, and I was pretty sure my employer wouldn't give a shit, so I decided to handle it. That brought on another set of questions — how to do just that? Do I nab one of the amateur trackers or do I wait for their move? The narrow bench began to dig into my ass, so I made a decision. I would go about my business and wait to be followed again.

# CHAPTER THREE

When I left the gym, I navigated the streets in the same way that I had after leaving the restaurant. I crossed the street several times and used the bright storefront windows to see what was behind me. I moved through the city entering different stores and shops so that I could look out and see if any faces looked familiar. After two hours the exercise seemed futile — I couldn't find a tail, and the sun was lowering into the west. I needed to rest, but I didn't want to go back to the office — it would be an obvious place to pick me up again. I decided to leave the car there, and took a cab to Jackson Square, a downtown mall that shared its lower level with a farmers' market. I moved out of the cab and paid quickly, using a ten for a four-dollar fare. I moved into the market and let the crowds wash over me. I followed their pull and moved with the throngs of people looking for fresh food to bring home at a price better than the supermarkets. At six in the evening, the market was perfect: there were dozens of exits and hundreds of people. It was a nightmare for tailing someone. I randomly made my way through the market until I saw a bus pull up at a stop just outside one of the exits. I walked casually out the door and on to the bus just before its doors closed.

The bus lurched ahead and the damp musk of the people hit my senses like a sucker punch. My nose was flooded with the different smells of people and the wares they had bought at the market. I found a lone seat and sat reading a bus pamphlet and planning my way home.

Home was a place I rarely used. It was mine in name, and had been my home for more than a dozen years. My parents had never lived there, and I had shared it with my uncle for only a handful of years.

When I was a child, three or four times a year my parents would tell me they had to work, and it was best I stay with family. I never knew at the time what my parents did. I never thought about why they only "worked" a few weeks out of the year. I learned about it all after the day they went to work and never came back.

During the "work" years my uncle watched over me at his house without comment or complaint. He wasn't an unpleasant or mean man; he was just quiet. He sent me to school, made my meals, and made sure I did my homework. He also left a book for me to read, every day, on the shelf beside the door. It was my job to come home, do my homework, and then read until my uncle arrived home to make dinner. The dinner conversations about books were the only way we developed a relationship. As we ate dinner, I told him about what I had read, and he asked me questions. He taught me the first lessons in my first real education. I learned to see beneath the surface — to look at what was going on under the current.

After a three-week stay in the fall, my uncle left me alone for a weekend. He said he had some work of his own to do and that he would be back soon. When he came back two days later, he had most of my things with him. I knew exactly what had happened when I saw him come through the door with two arms full of what I owned. My uncle told me there had been an accident, and that my parents had died on the way home to see me. It was here that the education given to me by my uncle first paid dividends. I looked through what my uncle told me; I saw all that was said in 3 D. I asked questions, many questions, and all of them were the right kind: Where was the accident? Where is the funeral? How do we bring the bodies home? It was a moment I would never forget. My uncle stared at me for what felt like hours, and then the side of his mouth turned up in a cold grin. The grin scared me because of all it said, and how unable I was to decipher it. All of the questions and probing I learned from my uncle at the dinner table fell apart when I was faced with an unspeaking grin that told me I didn't know enough.

My uncle sat me down and told me for the first time what my parents did for work. "They took things that didn't belong to them," he said.

"They were bad? Like bad guys?" I asked, and immediately I hated myself for betraying my immaturity by thinking of things in terms of cops and robbers.

"They weren't bad people, but they did take things. They never hurt anyone. They only took from people with a lot of money and a lot of insurance. Do you know what insurance is?"

"Yeah."

"So nobody ever got hurt."

It was my turn. My mouth turned up at the corner just like his. I mirrored the grin until he got it. "Yeah," he said softly, looking at me. "Two people got hurt."

Weeks later, I got up the courage to ask my uncle the

question that had been on my mind since the day he returned laden with all of my worldly possessions. "Uncle Rick, are you like my mom and dad?" I asked quietly across the dinner table. My mouth was dry with the paste of overcooked potatoes.

"No," was the only answer I got back at first. There was a long silence, and then the sound of chewing and swallowing. My uncle looked at me after he drank some of his milk. "Your mom and dad tried to be nice. They didn't want to hurt people, so they robbed businesses that had money and insurance. They had good hearts."

"But you steal things too, right? You're like them."

Anger flashed across my uncle's face for a second. "Damn it, Will! Don't you listen to me? They were good people. People can do the same thing, live in the same city, come from the same family. It don't make them the same."

My uncle went back to eating, and for a time I did too. I had made him angry. It wasn't talking about my parents that did it; it was asking about what he did. I ate more dry potatoes and decided to risk another question. "What do you do?"

There was no anger this time. "Kid, what I do is worlds apart from your mom and dad. I work all over, with different people, and I don't always do the same type of jobs. Now finish your dinner."

We didn't speak about the subject again for two years. I went to school and my uncle worked long, sporadic hours. Finally, years after I had moved in permanently, I spoke up again at the dinner table. As my uncle chewed a piece of leftover pork chop, I looked him in the eye and said, "I want to work."

My uncle didn't bat an eye at me or wait to swallow. "I know the guy who runs the Mac's Milk down the road. Maybe I get can get you a job as a stock boy."

"I want to do what my parents did. What you do," I said.

My uncle put down his knife and fork and looked me in the eye. "What the fuck, boy, you think it's the family business? Your parents weren't Robin Hood and Maid goddamn Marian. They were criminals. They did bad things, and it got them killed." He breathed deep in and out of his nose, and both of his hands gripped the table, his knuckles white. After a few moments he relaxed, took a drink of milk out of his glass, and spoke. "Your parents didn't want this life for you, kid. That's why they went after big scores with big risks. They wanted to raise you right. They wanted you to live in a house, have friends, and go to school. They wanted to be the Cleavers and you were supposed to be the Beav. But all that risk caught up with them. No one can do that work forever; it just doesn't have longevity. No, that life isn't for you. You need to be what they wanted you to be — a normal kid."

"I need to know," was all I could get out at first, in a weak voice. "I need to know them."

My uncle looked at me, and his face softened almost imperceptibly. "Kid, they were your parents —"

"No," I interrupted, my voice gaining strength. "I didn't know them. I didn't know what they did, or why they did it. They never let me in on that, and now they never can. They raised me and loved me but they were never real. I need to know them. I need to know what they did. I want to work."

My uncle stared at me for a good long time, and just like countless times before, the corner of his mouth raised into a cold grin. The grin made me unsure of myself and what I wanted, but I held strong. I stared at the grin and said nothing; I fought every urge I had to turn away until he spoke.

"I can't turn you into them or what they were. They got killed for being themselves and doing what they did. The best I can do, kid, is show you what I do. You'll see the world they lived in, but you'll survive because you'll follow my rules. That's the best I can do."

"Okay," I said. I fought my lips but they moved on their own. I grinned at my uncle for about two seconds until his palm crashed into my cheek.

I was on the floor when the burning in my cheek was joined by a ringing in my ears. I looked up, and my uncle stood over me. "Smiling and laughing gets left in the schoolyard. You just left that all behind when you asked for a job. You're not going to like it and you're probably going to hate me for it, but I'll teach you. You're in for a rough patch, kid. Now get up."

I stayed on the ground for a second and stared at the figure above me. Then I got up, watching his shoes, then shins, belt, shirt, and finally his face. I let the grin I had seen so many times before form on my face. I knew it looked like his; I had practised it enough to know. My cold grin was not startling to my uncle; if anything it startled me when it was returned in kind. I was startled for about two seconds by my uncle's response — then his fist came into view, and the lights went out.

# CHAPTER FOUR

After several transfers, I was a few blocks from the house. I walked towards it, conscious of the sounds created by the city and the night. In the glow of the streetlights I saw eyes watching me inches from the ground, but I saw no human eyes tracking my movements. I walked through the open gate in front of the house. Junk mail had been crammed into the mailbox by several companies that already thought I could be a winner. I unlocked the door, fighting the stiffness of the old mechanism. Its age made it turn with a groan, and I hoped, as usual, that the key would not break off. Inside the air was stale. The house had no real smell to speak of, probably because the house had no tenants to speak of.

I raided the kitchen looking for unspoiled food and found very little to choose from. I found crackers and an old jar of peanut butter that had given up its oil to the surface. I stirred the peanut butter with a knife and ate it with the crackers while I cleaned my Glock. When I finished with the Glock, I pulled my spare piece, a SIG Sauer 9 mm, from a compartment under the floorboards, and cleaned that as well. The amateurs I had met hadn't seemed like the fighting type, but then again they didn't seem like the type that would be able to find me, either. I decided I wouldn't let them surprise me again.

The next morning I used two buses and a cab to get me back to the office by nine. The Glock was in a holster at the small of my back; I placed the SIG in a holster taped to the underside of the desktop. I made a cup of tea and rolled my chair to the window to read the paper. Between stories, I glanced at the street below, looking for things that stood out. After I had read a story about local rezoning, I looked down to see a car pull up in front of the building. Three men got out of the car; each was dressed in a trench coat and sunglasses. The car screeched away once the three were clear, its tires spinning until smoke poured out. The car disappeared around a corner amidst the screams of pedestrians and the horns of other motorists.

These guys were absolutely unbelievable. I pulled the gun from the holster at my back and racked a round into the chamber. I put the Glock, safety off, in my lap, and waited.

In two minutes, there was a knock at the office door. I didn't move. Thirty seconds passed, and I saw a face pressed to the frosted glass. Another knock. I put my hand on the gun in my lap and yelled, "Just a minute, I'm in the john."

Another ten seconds passed and then the door opened slowly. The first one through eyed my grin with amazement. He stood inside the doorway staring at me until I waved him in, saying, "Come on inside." He was regular height with black hair that stood up in the front. The hair was sloppy over the ears, and I imagined it had been some months since he had a haircut. His nose was pointed like a beak, and his face was unshaven. A belly created a bulge

MIKE KNOWLES

under the buttoned trench coat he wore. The other two men tried to enter together, the larger finally managing to squeeze through first. He was bigger than chubby, but not yet obese. He had close-cropped red hair with a goatee to match, and on his left hand skin cream had dried crusty white. The third guy was tall, well over six feet, rail-thin, with a ponytail tied loose. He had circular John Lennon style glasses on a small pointed nose, and an Adam's apple that protruded from his neck. I presumed that the one who entered first was the leader, because he was the one to speak first — unsurely, but first.

"Uh . . ." he said.

I cut him off. "There's no name on the door, and no office number, so I know you don't want anything honest. Just spit out what you really came here for."

The three men shared a look, and then it started. The two at the back pulled at their coats and began to produce guns. The whole process took several seconds because of the time the stubborn snaps on their coats took to open. I could have shot all three using either gun, but I let it play out. Two guns, big ones, were aimed at my face. On the right side of two guns, the talker lost all of his nervousness and began to question me.

"Where the fuck is the bag, you motherfucker? I'll kill your ass dead if you don't talk, fucker!"

Amateurs always thought hard-asses spoke like that. I played along. "What bag?"

"You know exactly what bag. The one you took off Nicky at the airport."

"I'm sorry," I said calmly. "You must have me confused with someone else."

The leader fumbled under his coat, brought out a piece of paper, and slammed it onto the desk. I stared at it while the sweat from his palm dried off the surface of the glossy paper. It was a picture of me leaving the airport with the bag. The image was grainy, but it was me. The photo had several numbers in each corner, as though the shot came from a security camera. This was the first time I was impressed. They had a watcher, someone I didn't see, use the airport security cameras to get a shot of me coming from the bathroom.

"Well, it seems like I've been found, but you're late — the bag's gone."

"We know that, fucker! We want it back."

I filed the fact that they knew the bag was gone away in my brain, along with the name of the guy at the airport, which they had let slip. "Can't help you. The bag's been picked up," I said.

"By who?"

I knew something they didn't. It felt good to score a point against them after they had shown up knowing about me and the transfer of the bag. "You don't want to know. They wanted the bag. They got it. You candy-asses couldn't hang with them, so let it go. You lost the bag, but you're alive."

"Candy-asses, candy-asses, you fuck . . . fuck. I'll show you." The words sputtered out of his mouth as he twisted around to the fat one behind him. He wrestled the gun out of the fat man's hand and aimed it at my head from three feet away. His hands were shaking with rage, but at that range it didn't really matter; he could hit me no matter how much the barrel trembled. He held the gun with two hands and used both of his thumbs to pull back the hammer. I fought all the urges of fear and stared into his eyes. Time began to stretch; seconds felt like minutes, but everything snapped back when the skinny gunman with the Lennon glasses spoke up.

"Relax, Mike, we need this guy alive," he said.

Mike took a few seconds, and then pulled the gun away and gave it back to the heavier of the two men.

"We found you, you fuck. We know who you are. We want the bag back and if we don't get it, we'll get you," Mike said.

"I told you the deal is done. I'm a middleman, nothing more."

"You have a day. Let's go," Mike said, and the three of them turned their backs and left. Mike went first, followed by skinny, then fat. They took turns this time so no one got stuck. I sat there thinking about how they had turned their backs on me. I could have pulled out a gun from anywhere and shot them dead, but the amateurs didn't know that. One question rolled through my mind: how did these amateurs do such a pro job of finding me?

I sat in my chair and stared straight ahead. My whole lower body was damp with sweat. I spent twenty seconds like that, then I turned to the window. After a minute, I saw the three get into the black sedan they arrived in. As soon as they were in, the car peeled out from in front of the building. From the height and angle of my window, I only managed to make out an "H" on the far left of the plate, but I knew the vehicle: it was an Audi. The shape had been imperfectly copied by several American and Japanese automakers, but there was no mistaking the look of a real Audi sedan. I went to my desk and pulled a pad and pen from the second drawer on the left. I wrote down the information I had so far: the bagman named Nicky, descriptions of Mike and his two friends, the make of the car, and the "H" I saw on the licence plate. I tore the sheet from the pad, and stashed the information in a locked file cabinet with my paid bills.

I sat back in the chair and considered my options, which weren't many. The bag wasn't coming back willingly, so I could either try to find my new friends or wait for them to come to me again. I knew nothing about the bag or the people I took it from. I needed to know what I was up against before I made a move. In the end, I decided to make a call to the boss. Maybe he would give me an idea about who was on to me. I picked up the cell phone and dialled the same unlisted number I had called yesterday. It was the number for a restaurant, which it was, among other things. I waited, listening to the ringing tones. Promptly after the second chime, the phone was answered.

"Yeah?"

"I need an audience with the man," I said.

"I think you have the wrong number. This is a restaurant."

"Just tell him I delivered his bag and I just realized that there's some other luggage that needs to be dealt with." I didn't wait for the guy on the other end to hang up first because I knew it was coming. The message would be automatically passed on and the right people would know what it meant. I figured I had some time before my question was answered, so I made a run to the deli at the corner. I picked up four large crusty rolls along with slices of pastrami, salami, corned beef, and turkey. I also got milk, a couple of deli pickles, and three pickled eggs. I took the food up to the office and set it in the small fridge I had in the corner. I pulled a book from a desk drawer and began to read with my feet on the windowsill.

I had finished two sandwiches and a pickle when I heard the steps. I dog-eared my page and gripped the SIG in the holster fastened under the desk. The room dimmed as a large shape blocked the light coming through the frosted glass of the door. I kept one hand on the gun and picked up an egg with the other hand as Julian walked into the room without knocking. He took a seat in the chair across from me and stared. I stared back at him and ate my egg.

"The job was done. You did what you were supposed to do. Everything was finished. Why the call?"

"This morning the bag owners were here looking for the bag," I said, in between small bites of the egg.

Julian stared. If he cared he didn't show it. "So? What's your point? How is this our problem?"

Julian's slow, repetitive style had a way of cutting through bullshit. "Point is, Julian, I need to know some things."

"So? What's your point? How is this our problem?" The mastodon in front of me altered. His tone changed; he was no longer polite, no longer a pleasant associate. He was considering what would have to be done about me.

I popped the last of the egg into my mouth and chewed. After I swallowed, I took a sip of milk, never moving my eyes away from Julian's. "I want to know who the clients are, what they want back, and any other information I can get," I said.

Without a word Julian rose from his chair and left. I wasn't surprised he would go and consult with Paolo. Julian was important but he wasn't management. I made a third sandwich and cursed under my breath; I had forgotten to get cheese. About ten minutes passed before the same shadow loomed in the doorway. Julian came in without knocking, again, and sat in the chair he had just left. I held the sandwich with my left hand, keeping my right below the desk on the gun. I took a bite and returned the look Julian was giving me.

"Well?"

"The boss says he's disappointed. He's angry about what you've done. He's not happy. He says he used you because he didn't want any complications. I told him we should just cut off the contact point — you. You know, kill you. But the boss said to give you some time to handle the problem."

"How long?"

"Two days. Forty-eight hours."

"Two days. Fine. What can you tell me?"

"The owners of the bag were computer nerds. They were moving something the boss wanted."

Computer nerds. That explained the photo from an airport surveillance camera. One of them must of hacked into the security feed. "Why use me? Why not you?"

"There had to be deniability. No one could know who was interested. It was supposed to be anonymous. But you fucked that up, eh, tough guy?"

I let his challenge go unanswered and continued to probe. "What was in the bag?"

"None of your business. You don't need to know. Next question."

"How did you find out about these computer nerds?"

"None of your business. You don't need to know. Next question."

"What else can you tell me, Julian?"

"Two things. The first is an address, twenty-two Hess. The second is I'll see you in two days." With that, the dinosaur was up and on his way to the door.

"Julian," I said. He turned to face me, his bulk erasing the door, and stared for a long minute. I put the last bite of sandwich in my mouth and raised my index finger and thumb. I felt a familiar grin pull at the side of my mouth and I dropped my thumb. It didn't scare him; he didn't even seem to notice. He stood in the doorway for ten long seconds, showing zero emotion; then he left. I went to the file cabinet and retrieved the notes I had taken earlier. "Computer nerd" and "22 Hess" were all I could add to the random details I had collected. I thought about the bag I had taken from Nicky. Paolo used me because he wanted to insulate himself. No one was to know about the contents of the bag or that he was interested in it. Since no one outside of Julian knew that I worked for Paolo, having me steal the bag was the best way to make it look like he wasn't involved. The contents of the bag had something to do with computers, which meant it was probably still around in some form or another. Software is worth something, but it's not like drugs or cash; it doesn't vanish, and it isn't consumed and can't be laundered. The information that was on whatever was in the bag must have been of interest to Paolo. But what kind of information could a bunch of amateurs have that would interest a man like Paolo Donati?

I leaned back in my chair and stared at nothing in particular. Whatever the contents of the bag, I had two days and few options. I could steal the package back from Paolo and spend my life looking over my shoulder, or I could get the amateurs off my back. It took only seconds to weigh it out: I had to visit 22 Hess and the boys who paid me a visit earlier.

It was still early in the day, only ten past one. I pulled a short-sleeved oxford-cloth shirt from the small office closet and put it on. The blue shirt had a faded pattern and it blended into a crowd well. I left the shirt untucked over my jeans and left the office. I got in the car, tossed the Glock into the glove box, gunned the engine hard, and drove fast away from the office, keeping a close eye on the mirror for a tail. As I made the different lefts and rights, I noticed a black Audi cut in front of me from a side street. It stayed with me until I made another turn, and a minute later it was ahead of me again. These assholes were unbelievable. They were doing a tail in front of me — which only works on long roads with few turnoffs — and they were using the same car they had driven to the office earlier. I pulled a pen from the glove box and wrote down the rest of the plate, H21 2T5, on my forearm. When I saw an opening, I made a U-turn from the far right lane to the far left. As I pushed the car through traffic, weaving tightly around other motorists, I heard the sounds of horns. I watched the Audi in the rear-view attempt a similar U-turn only to get blocked in the middle of the street.

I made my way alone to 22 Hess with little trouble after that. The neighbourhood housed pubs and restaurants, a dentist, a tattoo parlour, and other businesses. The road on this portion of Hess Street was brick instead of pavement, and each of the buildings was set back from the street; they all had ample front gardens or patios. The building I wanted was a two-storey walk-up that had no use for its patio, so the space had been converted into a small garden with a black iron fence and several benches for smoking employees. The building looked as if it had begun life as a house, but it had been recently modernized for a different type of clientele. The large window that faced the street had been re-paned with reflective glass that deflected the sunlight onto the garden.

I parked across the street and watched the building. For twenty-five minutes nothing stirred; no one went in or came out. The pedestrian traffic was light. Most of the crowds were probably going back to work after their lunch. The occasional person walked by my car but none of them were police or security. The length of time in which nothing happened made me think I would be able to meet with these boys without being disturbed. I pulled the Glock from the glove box and made sure it was loaded and ready. I shifted in my seat and tucked the gun under my shirt into the holster at the small of my back.

Once I was armed, I got out and fed the meter two quarters, earning me half an hour. I wasn't going to be long, but parking tickets lead to paper trails, and people can follow those trails. I opened the Volvo's trunk and pulled out a baseball cap, which I pulled low over my eyes while I waited for a break in the traffic. The second to last car before the light turned was a police car. I smiled at the cop in the passenger seat as he rolled by. He stared back uninterested. When the street was clear, I crossed and followed the path of the police car. The patrol car turned left at the next lights, and neither of the two men inside looked back at me. Seeing the police car didn't bother me. I had been on Hess Street for half an hour and it was the first sign of the law I had come across. I figured I had at least a half of an hour before the police would be back; that was twenty minutes more than I needed.

I doubled back up the street and walked through the garden with my hat still pulled low. When I opened the front door, I was greeted with the smell of recycled office air. Fifteen feet in front of me was a receptionist speaking into a headset. The woman seated behind the desk was plump, almost round. Her nose was pointed up in a slightly piggish way, and her round face was accentuated by a curly mass of short hair. She occupied her free hands with a bottle of red nail polish. I angled my head low so that the visor of the hat hid my features from any cameras above me. I couldn't be sure who knew me in the building, and I didn't want any new friends. I waited politely in front of the receptionist, looking at the counter, the floor, and the two hallways leading away from the reception desk. The hallway ahead had only one door I could see; its wood was polished and expensive. The hallway to my left contained several doors, each with plastic name plates beside them.

The receptionist finally told someone to hold on and greeted me cheerfully: "How may I help you today, sir?" It was said without any hint of sarcasm or feeling. It was an automatic response to a visitor.

I smiled pleasantly. "Hey, is Mike around?" I said, using the name the amateur let slip in my office.

She spoke again with congenial efficiency. "Just a moment, sir, let me check to see if he is available." She touched a button and spoke into the headset. "Mr. Naismith," she chirped, "you have a visitor who would like to see you." There was a pause and then the woman said, "No." She looked at me again, and I smiled before turning my head to look at the art hanging on the walls. I heard her say, "Not by me, sir," before ending the call with a "yes, sir."

She looked at me and said Mr. Naismith would be out momentarily to see me. I decided to chance it and asked the receptionist, "Is Mikey's office still around the corner there?"

The receptionist craned her neck, her eyes following my pointing finger down the left hall, and said, "Um, no. That is where our associates work. Mr. Naismith's office is the door in other hallway."

I thanked her and started down the hall. I heard a protest of, "Hey, you can't do that!" But I kept on walking. As I neared the door, I could hear a buzz and the sound of the receptionist calling from her desk to inform Mr. Naismith about my behaviour. I opened the expensive door without slowing down.

Mike was bent over his desk, his back to me, speaking into the intercom. It must have buzzed as he walked to the door, and he had reached over his desk to answer the call. He had just enough time to look over his shoulder and see me before I pulled his hand off the buzzer and punched him in the kidney. My arm was around his neck before he had a chance to slump to the floor.

I spoke into his ear calmly and clearly. "Tell the girl at the desk that everything is cool. Tell her we went to school together and I was trying to surprise you." When I said the last few words I squeezed his throat for emphasis. "Anything funny and you'll be dead before you hit the floor. The receptionist will be next, way before she gets from nine to one one on the phone."

I reached over and held down the speak button on the intercom. Mike laboured out, "It's okay, Martha, my friend just wanted to surprise me . . . I . . . I haven't seen this guy since high school. Please just hold my calls." There was a small grunt of pain in between breaths, but he got out what I wanted him to say.

"Yes, sir, Mr. Naismith." The receptionist sounded like she wasn't convinced, but she was in no position to question. She clicked off the line and went back to work.

I kept the choke on and squeezed until the man I now knew as Mike Naismith brought his hands up to pull on my arm. I seized the opportunity and let the choke go in favour of a wrist hold. I pinned him to the desk with his head beside a paperweight and his arm ninety degrees in the air.

"Now," I said, "it's time we had a talk without guns being pointed at people."

"How did you find me?" All the bravado and tough language from before had left when I hit him.

"Do you think it was that hard? You're an amateur and I'm a pro. Finding you is a slow morning. I want to know how you found me."

There was a long pause before Mike grunted. "We followed you."

I twisted his arm, feeling bone scrape on bone. "All

right, all right," he said. "The bag had a GPS. We tracked it."

There was a new world dawning while I slept. A GPS tracker let these amateurs follow me home, and I didn't do a thing about it. I should have got rid of the bag right away, but I was told to deliver it. I assumed the bag was clean because, before now, every bag I delivered had been clean. I hated myself for five seconds, then I got back to work.

"Now, what did I take from you?" I figured identifying the package would give me some info on how bad the situation was. I had to find out how far these guys would go to get the bag back, and what it would take to persuade them to give up. Everything depended on the bag. Mike gave me no response, so I pushed the arm to ninety-five degrees and asked again. "What did I take?" I felt the last few degrees produce another grinding sensation deep in Mike's shoulder. His arm was so far back he was unable to offer any fight against the hold. Any more pressure from me and his shoulder would start splintering apart like old wood under too much tension.

"It was disks, that's all — disks. Goddamn it! You're breaking my arm!"

"What was on the disks? And who were they going to?"

I heard Mike breathe heavily in and out, and I listened to him groan. He was trying to raise his chest off the desk to relieve the pressure on his shoulder, but the position he was in gave him no leverage or muscle power.

"Answer me before I make you, Mike. Either way I win. If we do this fast you might even get out of a trip to emergency."

"It was the files we took; all of them. We don't have anything else."

Mike was starting to scream, and I was starting to realize that he had no idea who I was working for. I spun him around using the arm as a lever and laid my fist right into his stomach. Under his wrinkled untucked dress shirt was a soft belly, the kind you get from sitting a lot and eating at your desk every day. He wheezed like a balloon deflating, then slumped into a fetal position.

"I could do without the yelling. From this point on," I told him, "I want you to act like I'm new to all of this. Explain it to me step by step, or this will take a lot longer than you could ever want it to."

Mike lay like a fish pulled into a canoe; he gasped and struggled and before long he started to sob. I waited five seconds and then pulled him up to his seat by his greasy wax-styled hair. I showed a deliberate wind-up, and Mike gasped. I stopped the punch halfway to his face and asked again, "Will you tell me everything?"

"Yuh, yuh . . . yes." He sobbed. Snot ran down his face.

"What was it I stole?"

It took several seconds for the question to register. I had to wait several more while Mike wondered how I couldn't know what I took. I decided to make things easy on us both. "I'm only pick-up and delivery, like FedEx. I don't know contents. I usually don't ask questions, but now that there are complications I want to know everything, and you are the only source of information I have."

Mike's breath came back during my little speech. His voice was less shaky, and the tears on his face had absorbed into his collar. "It was accounting records, all right?"

"Were they yours?"

"No. They belonged to someone else. We were selling them back."

I exhaled loudly and turned to the door. The turn masked my arm moving, and when I turned back I used my hips to power a left hook into the side of Mike's neck.

My fist hit the meat of his neck — right in between where his stubble stopped and the hair on the back of his neck began. I didn't hit him too hard, just enough to shock and scare. The impact, and fright, drove him out of his chair.

As he sputtered on the floor, I crouched down beside him and said, "Listen, Mike, I don't have all day and I don't want you to keep holding out on me until I ask just the right questions. Tell me everything, and I mean everything."

Mike got out a, "You asshole," between sobs.

I put him back into his chair and asked once again, "Last time. Tell me everything about the disks."

He gulped in air. Then he began spitting out information almost faster than I could listen. "We repair computers here. One day an accountant, at least we think he's an accountant, came in with his laptop. He was totally freaking out. I mean really losing it. He said he had lost some files and he needed them back pronto. He said he would pay anything — it just had to be done immediately. We took his laptop and gave it a full diagnostic check. Its hard drive still had copies stored from before the system crash. While we were restoring the files, we took a peek to see what was so important. It was all accounting files, with client names, company names, and bank account numbers. Some of the banks were offshore banks. Jimmy, one of the boys on staff, he was able to understand the information. He was an accountant before he came here. He saw . . . mistakes; he realized a lot of the information wasn't kosher. It took us a whole day to figure out what was hiding in the files. Once we had the scam figured, we made encrypted copies of the files, erased the originals, and then called the accountant to set up a trade. Heh, he said he'd give anything, right? We gave him a number, and he said he needed three days to pony up the dough. We said okay, and three days later we set up an exchange."

"At the airport. That was what I took off Nicky." I was beginning to see where this was going.

Mike seemed genuinely surprised that I knew Nicky's name; he must have not realized that he let it slip when we first met. The only part I couldn't figure out was how Paolo Donati fit in, and more important, why did he care about blackmailing an accountant?

"What's Nicky's last name?" I asked.

"Why?"

I pulled back my fist, and Mike barked a quick answer. "Didiodato," he said.

"Whose idea was it for him to be the bagman?"

"Bagman?"

"The guy who took the disks to the airport."

"Oh. He volunteered. No one here has ever done anything like this before, so no one argued with him."

I wondered why a kid who worked with computers all day would want to be the face of a blackmailing scam. Why would anyone volunteer to put themselves out there like that? I didn't allow myself to focus on any theories for too long; I had been in the office almost ten minutes. "Who did the accounting files belong to?" I asked.

Mike didn't answer. He shook his head twice, gritting his teeth, showing the first sign of backbone, or of a fear of something worse than me. I hit him in the stomach, and sound echoed off the walls. The sound wasn't my fist. The loud crack was something else, and it turned both our eyes to the door. Then the screaming started.

# CHAPTER FIVE

Over the screaming, automatic gunfire erupted in the halls. Less than a second later, the heavy office door burst inward. The door was replaced by a more solid figure. I turned my hips to hide some of the movement of my arm — which was already reaching behind my back. But as I moved, the giant in the doorway raised a gloved hand. In his fist was a huge gun. He said only one heavily accented word. "Don't."

I didn't know why he hadn't shot me, but I didn't waste time on it. I locked eyes with the giant and waited. If he minded me eyeing him, he didn't show it. His gun was pointed at me, but every now and then he glanced to look at Mike — who was pretty messy from our conversation. He never asked Mike if he was okay, so I ruled out the giant being Mike's backup. The giant's glances were brief and allowed me no chance to move.

I stared at the giant and took in every detail. He was over six and a half feet tall, with short blond hair shaved close to his head. He had the shoulders of a man who swung a hammer all day. His face was young but worn, with the wrinkles and creases that come from being in the elements for extended periods. He was wearing a black nylon wind suit that he had zipped all the way up so that only a portion of the collared shirt he wore underneath peeked out. I stared at the outfit, intrigued by the contrast of a formal shirt with such a casual jacket. It was then that I noticed the gloves and shoes. The gloves were black latex. The shoes were zipped inside rubber covers — the kind used to protect leather shoes from the snow. The outfit told me all I needed to know. Something bad was happening here. The kind of thing that can't leave evidence, and I was in the middle of it.

I ignored all of my instincts. I would not let my brain entertain all of the questions forming in my synapses. I dismissed the thoughts about who the giant was, what was going on in the hallway, and whether or not I would soon be dead. I thought only of drawing my gun. I replayed the thought over and over, imagining the smooth draw I would have to make in a split second. My concentration lapsed when gunfire popped in the hall again. There was screaming, more gunfire, and finally silence. The smell of cordite snuck into the room over the shoulders of the giant. He hadn't flinched at the sound of gunfire, and his head didn't turn away in curiosity.

*Fuck,* I thought. *Why doesn't he look?*

I heard a thumping getting louder and realized that it was the sound of running — in heels. A blur passed the door, visible only in the slivers of hallway that showed from behind the giant. He gave no sign of realizing that someone had passed. He kept his head still and his gun level at my chest. I heard a voice shout, "Ivan!" The giant didn't move at first. The name was called again — with a much louder voice. At once, the giant sprang to life like a carousel being turned on. He turned at the hip, moving the cannon away from my torso, and fired once down the hallway. His hips turned back, but his gun was already on its way to the floor as the echo of my Glock bounced off the walls. My gunshot had mingled with his, making it inaudible outside the room.

The bullet entered his right shoulder at a point where there was minimal muscle mass. I was lucky with the shot because a few inches either way would have hit the dense muscle of a deltoid or a pectoral, and would not have done the job. Ivan acknowledged the pain with one small grunt and then he immediately began to bend for his gun, which had pitched forward into the room.

"Easy, big man, or the next one is in the head," I said.

The blood trailed down the nylon windbreaker, gaining momentum because it wasn't absorbed, and dripped onto the floor beside his covered shoes. He was still, bent slightly at the waist, staring at the gun on the floor.

"Leave the gun on the floor, step slowly into the room, and sit in the green chair, Ivan," I said calmly.

Ivan did as he was told, as though the idea was a direct command he could not disobey. He sat in the client chair in front of the bookcase; the chair angled toward Mike's desk and away from the doorway.

"Mike, take a seat behind your desk," I said.

"What the hell is going on out there? I can't stay here. I gotta go now. I gotta go. I gotta —" I smacked him hard with my left hand, and he staggered to his desk without any further complaint. I moved to the side of the desk, putting my back to the wall. It looked like I was watching a face-to-face meeting take place between Ivan and Mike. Mike's tears and Ivan's clenched jaw made the meeting appear extremely tense.

"Talk and you're dead, partner," I said to Ivan. If he

heard me, he didn't let it show. Shock was probably setting in, or the monster was alive behind those eyes waiting, visualizing, just as I was. Mike looked back and forth nervously. Sweat had wet the waxed hair on the top of his head and it was starting to wilt. The shooting down the hall had him shocked and scared. His eyes looked at me as his head swivelled from the door back to Ivan. His mouth was open slightly as though his tongue was too big to fit into a closed mouth.

"Shut up, Mike," I said. "If you make this harder than it has to be, I'll put you down too." He sensed how serious I was, and his open mouth closed.

With Mike silent, I ran through ways to get out of 22 Hess. Mike's office had no windows to jump out of, and running down the hall had a lousy track record. I had to wait for an opportunity and take it when it came.

I picked up Ivan's gun from the floor and admired the size and weight of it; the Colt Python is only a bit smaller than a cannon. The gun was missing only the one round it took to kill the woman who ran for her life down the hall. I held the Colt down at the side of my leg with my left hand, out of fear that it would pull my pants down if I put it under my belt. I listened as the clock above the door clicked second by second one hundred eighty times. From the halls, I heard doors opening and closing, mumbled voices, and the occasional laugh. I knew the safety of the room would vanish when the voices down the hall called for Ivan again. There were no opportunities coming. I had to move.

"Both of you, get up and move to the door. Step into the hall facing right."

Ivan mechanically stood and moved toward the door, one arm immobile as he walked. Mike shuddered and stayed put in his chair.

"Get up, Mike, or I leave you here."

My words broke through whatever mental fog Mike was in, and he got up. He moved in Ivan's direction, but kept his distance from the big man as though he was afraid that the limp, wounded arm would come to life and strangle him. I moved around the desk until I was behind the two. I got close and pressed a muzzle into each man's neck while I spoke.

"Mike, is there an exit at the left end of the hall?"

"Yuh, yuh, yeah. It's around the corner at the end."

"How many steps?" I asked.

"What?"

"If you walked it, how many steps would it take?"

"I dunno, twenty-five or thirty."

"Okay, boys, we're going to back up twenty-five or thirty steps to the exit. Once we're there, Mike and I are out of here."

The giant moved as though he were a robot following a direct command. Mike moved beside him, dragged along by the giant's gravity. Mike suddenly realized how close he was to the Russian and tried to move back, but he changed his mind when he felt the muzzle of the Python in my hand separate two of his vertebrae. I moved backward, a step behind both men, down the empty hall to the exit. Ivan must have been sent alone to cover this hallway, which meant he was as real as he looked. As we moved, I whispered over Ivan's bad shoulder: "A bullet will drop you as easy as the girl. Remember that, big guy."

There was no response from Ivan — no twitch. He was waiting just like I had been, but I wasn't going to give him any opportunity to move. Using a low voice, I counted the steps back for each man. No one at the other end of the hall made any noise, and no one yelled down to Ivan. After fifteen paces, my heel touched the receptionist with

47

the freshly painted nails. She wasn't breathing. The Colt had put a hole through the centre of her back. The exit wound left the white walls tinged with pink.

"Step lightly over the girl and don't look down. Mike, I mean it."

Both men took a large step backwards over the body. Ivan looked straight ahead; Mike stole a glance at the body. "Oh, God, Martha!" he screamed.

The sound of Mike's voice bounced off the walls with a boom like bowling pins falling down. A loud, "What the fuck was that?" came from the end of the hall seventeen paces in front of me. The voice was gravelly, and it sounded Russian — the *w* in "what" sounded like a *v*.

"Steady, boys," I said, before counting steps eighteen and nineteen.

"Ivan!" a voice called. It sounded like "Eevan" from twenty paces away. I couldn't see who was speaking from the other end of the hall; I could only make out bits of images through the spaces between the two men.

"Keep moving. Don't stop." I shoved the guns hard into the two men as I said the word *stop*. We moved to the end of the hall as the voice repeated Ivan's name. After calling a second time, the voice clued in to what was happening and shouted something in a harsh language. We ignored the foreign command and kept walking.

"Stop!" The voice coming down the hall was loud and sounded like it was used to being obeyed. Out of instinct, all of us almost stopped. Ivan and I ignored the urge to comply and kept moving backwards. Mike, unable to disobey the voice at the end of the hall, stopped walking. He was falling before I heard the shot. It was low in the gut and it bent him over. Mike landed on his ass with a thump. His hands didn't break his fall because they were holding his stomach. I had five steps left. I raised both arms, pressed both guns into Ivan's back, and kept moving. I stopped counting out loud at twenty-seven, and after a silent twenty-eight and twenty-nine, Ivan made his move. He pancaked his huge body onto the floor, using his one good arm to break his fall. I dove left before a bullet could tear me in two at twenty-nine paces.

I hit the floor with my shoulder and rolled to my feet five paces from a grey metal door with a glowing exit sign on top. I pushed through the door and found myself in an alley. To my left were three metal stairs leading down to the pavement between 22 Hess and its neighbour. I leapt down the stairs and ran hard toward an overflowing Dumpster; I hooked around it, and kept running, invisible from the door I just exited. Once I was in the street, I crossed and entered another alley, which I followed to Queen Street. I went into the first coffee shop I saw and took a seat at the window. I waited for my breathing to slow before I got up to grab a newspaper and order a large tea. I flipped to the crossword and then scanned the room for a pen. I had to get up again to ask the girl behind the counter for something to write with.

"Do you have a pen I could use?"

"What for?" The girl's reply was cold, and she looked me dead in the eye as she said it. It was a challenge from a frumpy girl with hoops in her lip, nose, and eyebrow.

"I just wanted to do the crossword."

"That paper is for everyone, not just you."

I didn't think this meant no, because she didn't look away as though the conversation were over. "It's yesterday's paper," I said.

"It's still not yours."

"How much for the paper then?" I asked with a low, even tone. I didn't want any more attention than I had already gotten.

"We don't sell them."

She still didn't look away when she said this, making me still think we weren't done. "Did those hurt? The rings, I mean. In your face. Did they hurt?"

"No." Her voice was less sure; the conversation was getting away from her.

"Why three of them? Why not two? How do you decide what to pierce?"

"Why, you got a fetish?" Her tone was a bit more defiant. She thought she had scored a point in her little game.

"I just want to know why you need to make something out of nothing. Why do you need to pierce a lip, or an eyebrow? Why do you make nothing into a whole production? What I'm trying to say is, why do you want to hassle me for nothing? Or did I just answer my question? You can't leave things alone — not even your chubby lower lip."

She threw a pen at me, meaning to hit me in the face. I moved my head, and she hit a woman behind me who was drinking a latte. I picked up the pen as she said, "Ma'am, I'm so sorry. I didn't mean to . . ." I heard someone call for a manager as I took my seat and started writing. The crossword would explain my presence in the coffee house for an hour or two. I had no interest in the puzzle; I instead used it to chart out what I knew and what I didn't. I filled in the boxes of the puzzle with everything I had found out at 22 Hess. I worked fast, filling in names, places, and information I had learned. I noted everything Mike had told me about their piracy, and what I knew about the team that had shown up to clean the entire building. To the passerby I was not a person who was almost killed less than half an hour ago. I was a person who was very interested in his crossword puzzle. Over the two hours I stayed in the Second Cup, I recorded all of the information I knew, and the questions I had. I also learned the local bus route. My uncle hated writing anything down; he said it was the start of something concrete. Something a person could follow back to you. Most in my profession would have agreed with my uncle, but ever since I had lived with my uncle I did it. He taught me to dissect books before I learned to dissect people, and those early lessons were hard-wired into my brain. Seeing things on paper started my mind turning. I could swim through the information, picking out important details like a pike among minnows feeding on the biggest fish. It wasn't my uncle's way to use pen and paper, but it was something he could accept because his most important rule was to use whatever worked.

The names and accents I had heard at 22 Hess made me think I had crossed paths with the Russian mob. They had been a growing element in Southern Ontario for years, following Russian hockey players and circus troupes to Canada. The Russians were violent, but they were pros; they would make sure what happened to the computer geeks wouldn't attract the attention of the law for at least another few hours. I couldn't go back: they would have eyes posted there until the cops showed. Eventually the eyes outside would settle on my car, parked across the street from 22 Hess. The car didn't have my name on it, but the right people would track it to me eventually. I went to the coffee shop's pay phone and made a call to Sully's Tavern. The phone was answered on the second ring by a voice that was clear and without distortion.

"Hello?"

"It's Wilson."

"What is it?" The voice on the phone did not sound interested or concerned, but I knew better than to think Steve wasn't paying attention; he heard every word.

"I need you to do me a favour."

"What?" Mr. Personality was laying it on thick this afternoon.

"My car is over on Hess. I need it picked up."

"Is it hot yet?"

"No, but the cops will be checking it soon, so it needs to be moved fast."

"Where are you now?"

I told him, and listened to Steve chuckle. He seemed amused that I was stranded so close by.

MIKE KNOWLES

# CHAPTER SIX

Twenty minutes later, I was in Steve's car, a beat-up, decade-old Range Rover. The SUV was uncomfortable in the city, but ready to run forever. I was driving so Steve could do the quick pick-up. Never once did he ask why; he would do whatever I asked. I did Steve a favour once, and he'd been ready to help ever since. I always felt a pang of guilt asking him for help because I knew he'd always say yes. He would always help me for what I did, but I hadn't helped him for favours. I helped him because he had become like family in a time when I thought I would never have family again. I owed him as much as he owed me.

"Who's tending bar?"

"Sandra. With help from Ben," he said.

Since the day Sandra had been kidnapped, Steve always had Ben at the bar when he couldn't be, just to make sure things were kosher. Ben was way over six feet tall, and well over three hundred pounds. All of his size made him look like the son of a farmer, one who didn't own any machinery. It didn't help that he was one of the only men in the city who had overalls on regular rotation in his wardrobe. I had seen Ben take apart groups of people at once, but the real menace of the bar was Steve. He was no danger to the regular customers — just to those who were there to threaten his business or family, specifically Sandra.

At one time, I had been no more than a passing customer in the bar. I'd check into it once in a while for information and the like. One night I happened to brace a junkie a little hard, and Steve told me to let him go. I didn't listen because bartenders are usually full of hot air and Steve didn't look like much — he only weighed about one-seventy, and he could barely see through the hair that hung over his eyes. While I was holding the junkie to the wall with my forearm, I missed the sound of the thin bartender moving over the bar. Almost at once he was behind me, tripping me backward over his foot.

I bumped off the ground ready to fight. The junkie saw that Steve was between us and rushed out the door. Steve tilted his head forward, and with a hard jerk he sent his hair flying back. He used a rubber band from his wrist to tie the hair up into some kind of shabby samurai topknot. I threw a weak jab before he was done with his hair as a setup to something much worse; he surprised me, pulling my arm tight — hyperextending it. Steve twisted and pulled the arm in front of him and began pushing against it like he was at the turnstile to get on a roller coaster. I grabbed the brass rail on the bar and pulled against my arm, interrupting Steve's momentum. He stumbled into my field of vision, no longer able to put me to the floor. My elbow drove back over my shoulder and connected with his jaw, but it did nothing to loosen his grip. I hit him five more times in the jaw and side of the head until my twisted arm was free. The fight went on for three more minutes. Steve tried repeatedly to take me down while I tried to knock him out. I used fast hard punches and elbows out of fear of getting a limb broken in a painful joint lock.

After three minutes, we both were slow to get up and Sandra had just come back from the store. She walked up to the fight, unafraid, and pulled Steve away by the arm. At once, his eyes softened, and he followed her behind the bar. The junkie was long gone, and my left knee and right arm were severely stretched. I staggered to the bar and did the only thing I was able to do. I ordered a Coke.

We weren't friends after that, not by a long shot, but I did my best to respect the bar, and Steve did his best to turn an eye every now and then when I had to brace someone a little rough. Three years ago that all changed — not because of some touching Hallmark moment, but rather because of something much worse. We both got blood on our hands together. Blood has a way of making two people stick together like nothing else.

The neighbourhood where Sully's Tavern was located was rough. No one lived there because they wanted to — they just had nowhere else to go. Every violent offender, addict, and pedophile was like a magnet dragging others like them to the area. Sully's Tavern was the eye of the hurricane; it was the one peaceful spot in a mass of human depravity. The only real order in the neighbourhood came from Paolo's men. It was mob turf, and everybody was expected to pay into the local protection fund. The hoods in charge of the collecting left Steve alone for the first little while because his bar didn't turn a profit, and he didn't care who came in with who so long as they didn't start trouble. But when the bar started getting regular customers, the neighbourhood boys became more interested in Sully's Tavern. The first visit was on a Tuesday, then every other day after Steve refused to pay. The boys just didn't understand, being so low on the food chain and used to intimidating everyone, that Steve wasn't going to be scared into anything.

I heard rumblings of what was going on and I talked to Steve about it. "Those aren't punk kids, Steve, they work for a dangerous man. Just give them a piece of the pie and call it the price of doing business."

Quietly, under his hair, he said, "It's my business, my pie, no tastes. You want another Coke?"

I came in a week later, on a Monday, to find Steve ramming a man's head into the brass footrest of the bar. Another man was on the floor, his left arm and leg at unnatural angles. On the floor between the two men were baseball bats.

"What's going on?" I asked.

Steve paid no mind to my question as he finished with the hood. The gong sound of his skull hitting the hard metal was replaced by the sound of a skull falling into blood and teeth. The sound was like raw chicken falling off a counter onto the floor. Steve never once looked at me or said a word. His wiry body rippled under his thin white shirt as he grabbed each man by a foot. He didn't even flinch when one of the men began shrieking because Steve was pulling on the leg that was obviously damaged. Steve walked right past me, dragging the bodies into the street in front of the bar. As he walked back in he ran his fingers through his hair, removing the rubber band; his face once again becoming hidden.

"Time to put out new peanuts," was all he said to me.

I found out that night, through the grapevine, that the two men were collectors. After Steve's repeated refusals to pay, they had decided to step things up by coming into the bar with bats.

The next day, I went to the office and found Steve waiting

outside the door dressed in khakis and a white T-shirt. The veins in his forearms pressed out hard like overfilled balloons, and his hair was up in the topknot.

"Where can I find your boss?" was all he said.

I could see that he was ready to go through me to find out so I said, "Tell me."

Steve said he went for napkins, and when he came back Sandra was gone. A phone call came a few minutes after he walked in; it told him that to get his wife back he had to pay up all the "rent" he had missed. The kidnappers gave Steve three hours to get together all the money. Steve was no idiot; he knew that after what he'd done there was no way Sandra was coming back. He might get pieces of her, but she wouldn't be back as he knew her.

"The good thing is the time," I said. "They want the money so they'll keep her alive until they know they've got it. How much time is left?"

"Two hours." Steve's gaze was out the window; his fists were tight, clenching imaginary ghosts.

We left the office together and took my car downtown to Barton Street East; I parked in a public parking space, and we moved on foot over the pavement. The concrete had been repaved with chewing gum and cigarettes, making the rough surface smooth with urban grime. As we rounded the corner of an alley to Barton, its stream of people flowing by unyielding, I stopped and spoke to Steve. "This building around the corner — the barbershop — is the gate; Mario is middle management for some heavy hitters on the east side. Everything on the street goes through Mario. You do this and you are on everyone's radar."

Steve looked at me for about one second, long enough for me to see pure fury, pure hate. He turned and walked into the crowd, vanishing amid the faces. I followed, trying to keep up, but Steve moved fast, his thin body gliding through the human traffic. He entered the barber-shop without hesitation. As I followed in his wake, I eyed the barber pole spinning. I took a breath and thought about nothing, relaxing so I could commit to what I was about to become a part of. I was helping Steve, and back then I never once thought that I shouldn't — never once. I took one last look at the pole spinning white then red, and got ready for a lot more red.

When I opened the door the chime didn't turn any heads my way. Two barbers were unconscious on the floor. Beside the barbers lay a man in a finely tailored black suit. Six feet above his body was a fine spray of red on the white wall.

I moved through the room and into the next. The door to the office had been torn from one of the hinges; it hung on like a loose tooth. In the doorway, face down, arms cradling his head, lay another suit, dead. I could see the defensive wounds that had leaked onto the floor — Steve had come in slicing high. The pool of blood was growing; so were the screams inside the office. Steve wasn't talking; he was taking off Mario's ear with a barber's straight razor. He must have taken the razor off one of the barbers when he came in. Steve was using the razor like a conductor's wand, making the fat Italian man scream a bloody aria. His pockmarked face was made even uglier in its agonized distortion. The ear came off despite the pawing of stubby fingers. Steve slammed it on the desk and started on Mario's nose. When it was half off he looked at Mario and demanded, "Where is she?" The question had an exclamation point in the form of a haymaker.

When there was no response he moved the razor back to the nose, and the answers came like water from a faucet. "Tommy took her! He did it! Talarese did it, all right? Just stop!"

MIKE **KNOWLES**

"I know him," I said.

Mario saw me, and his eyes widened. "You fuck. You yellow traitor shit. I'll spit on your grave."

"Did you know?" Steve's voice was like a window breaking; it got everyone's attention.

Mario's eyes focused on Steve's, and he spit out hate camouflaged in English. "What did you expect when you acted like an animal. Everyone pays, everyone. Some just pay more than others." His last words were framed by a small smirk.

Steve stepped back and bent so that he was eye level with Mario. "Where does Tommy live?"

"Why?" Mario's smirk vanished, and he looked puzzled. I knew what he was thinking: no one would go looking for Tommy Talarese.

The nose came off with screaming and pleading, and then, once again, answers came. Tommy's mother, wife, and son lived in a red apartment building on King William Street. Tommy had made his home in the centre of the city, away from his bloody work on the east side. I knew the area. The building was one of several luxury complexes in the heart of downtown. The city tried to create upscale buildings, like Tommy's, that would offset the rapid decay of the city. Each building that went up pushed more people out. It was the city council's secret hope that they could move every undesirable citizen out of the city a block at a time — a transfusion of wealth to revitalize the decaying concrete. The lobby furniture in one of the complexes would be worth more than a year's rent in any of the older buildings in the area. The new buildings also had doormen working twenty-four hours a day to protect those with money from those without.

The sound of Steve's foot hitting the bloodied face followed the answers. The kick knocked Mario from the chair to the floor, and then the stomping started. The sound was like boots walking in thick mud. Steve stomped Mario long after he had died on the floor behind his desk. It would take the authorities some time to decipher what the mess on the floor was, and even longer to figure out who.

Back in the car, I didn't question what had happened — no one needed doubt. We moved through the streets fast and smooth. Neither of us spoke for the first few minutes. I was thinking about what Mario had told us. Tommy Talarese was as scary a human as I had ever met. He was a man who had gotten where he was through nights of blood. He revelled in cruelty as though it were a religion. Tommy had butchered entire families, raped children in front of their fathers, and tortured enough people to fill a cemetery. Tommy was a maniac of all trades, but he was especially fond of taking limbs. The east side was like a little Sierra Leone in the eyes of those who had come up against Tommy. He was out-of-his-mind crazy, and now he was interested in Steve.

"This Tommy Talarese," I said. "He's a big deal. He's Mario's boss, and a scary fuck in the truest sense of the words. He's sadistic and violent on a whole other level. He got where he is fighting with the Russians on the east side. He killed and killed like it was eating or breathing. There were battles in the streets years ago — the Russians tried to keep up with Tommy, and they almost did. Eventually some boundaries were organized, and the Russians got a piece of territory. Tommy was kept on the east side as a reminder of the way things used to be; the way they could be again. The problem is you. Why the hell is someone like him interested in you? Why is he pushing so hard to get rent from a bartender?"

Steve didn't say a word. His face and shirt were speck-led with blood, and he held the razor from the barbershop open on his thigh as he stared out the windshield. His voice eventually broke the white noise of traffic. "However this goes, you can always walk away. You try to stop me and I'll kill you." His voice never faltered. He never thought about it, or weighed out what he was telling me. He was saying what he was going to do; how it made me feel, and the problems I had with it, weren't going to change anything.

King William Street was lined with cars, so I double-parked outside number sixty-six, Tommy's building. Steve was out of the car before it stopped moving. I caught up with him at the front doors.

"Give me your gun," he said.

I gave Steve the Glock. He looked at it and asked if there was a round already in the chamber. I nodded, and we walked through the doors. Steve moved ahead, the gun hanging loosely in his hand. The doorman stood behind a counter protecting the tenants' mailboxes. He took one look at Steve's bloody face and reached for the phone. Steve walked behind the counter and kicked the back of the doorman's knee. The doorman slumped to his knees, his red trench coat becoming a dress on the ground. Steve turned the pistol around in one quick flip and hit the door-man on top of his cap.

I checked the doorman's book and found Talerese next to the number 5006. It was the highest number on the page. Talerese was on the top floor.

We got on the elevator and rode up side by side. I scanned for cameras, but saw none. The upscale building management must have thought the doorman was enough security. The elevator stopped just as a chime announced our arrival. We moved out and followed the direction arrow to apartment 5006. When we got to the door Steve knocked and waited. The knock was loud and authoritative.

A male voice said, "Who is it?" The voice was muffled, as though the man inside had his mouth full.

Steve knocked again. The voice barely got out, "I said who is —" before it was interrupted by Steve's boot kicking the door in. The door ripped through the lock and flew past the safety chain, knocking the owner of the voice to the floor. Steve fluidly moved through the door frame, firing a bullet as he crossed the entryway. Screams erupted like applause after the gun exploded. The bullet wasn't for the male voice; it was for the grandmother, the Nona, of the family. Mrs. Talarese — Tommy's wife — was shrieking as she rushed to the floor beside the body of the elderly woman. Steve quickly moved to the huddle of women on the floor and silenced the younger woman with a kick. The hard shin to the side of her head snapped her body onto the elderly woman already on the floor. The young man flattened by the door rolled to his feet and started to run at Steve. I grabbed him by the hair as he passed and yanked. His body, surprised and pained, straightened enough for me to loop an arm around his neck to hold him. Fuelled by rage, he strained against my body, pulling past the point of exhaustion. After forty-five seconds he was tapped, and his back slumped against my chest.

After the struggle was over, I had time to survey the situation. The son, a thin kid in his early twenties with a protruding Adam's apple, was hanging in my arms. Tears streamed his cheeks, and saliva hung in strands between his lips as he gasped for breath. He was like a mad dog surging against a chain on his neck, instinct forcing him to push against the yoke no matter the consequences. From the shape the side of his face was in, I could see he had already been worked over in a bad way. The other two occupants of the apartment lay huddled together. The grandmother was lying on her side near an overturned wicker chair and a toppled cane. Her white hair was thin and cut short. I could see her scalp through the strands surrounding her head. Her mouth was closed, and her chin sat higher on her face than it should have. She was old-world by the look of her. The old woman's toothless mouth would confirm her poor rural Italian heritage better than a birth certificate ever could. As she lay there unblinking, the centre of her blue dress bloomed a stain — one much darker than the light material of the dress. Tommy's wife moaned and held her rapidly bruising face as she recovered from the short kick she had received to the left side of her head. Her appearance was unlike her mother-in-law's. She was a petite woman, with a plain, unpretty face and large dark hair artificially expanded to twice its natural volume. The massive amount of jewellery on her hands and ears showed her to be far from the farm her mother-in-law grew up on a continent away.

Steve produced the razor from his pants and opened it slowly. The blade was black with the crusted blood that had pooled and dried while the razor was closed. The sight brought Tommy's wife to full attention.

"Where is the phone?" Steve asked.

No answers came from Maria's lips, so he slapped her hard across the face. When her head lolled back, Steve presented the question again, this time with the blade of the razor resting just under her nostrils.

"Call your husband and tell him what I have done."

Tommy's wife looked confused, but she did as she was told. She dialled the phone with shaking hands, softly whispering a prayer until someone picked up. "Tommy? It's Maria. Just listen. This guy just . . . just came here and shot Momma, and she's dead, and he hit me, and this guy he told me to call you. Help us! Please help us! I don't want to die, please, baby, please!"

The conversation turned into sobs and pleas. Steve took the phone from Maria. "Tommy, this is Steve. Sandra goes home now with you and she calls me when she's there. After she calls, you come home. Any tricks, and the boy and your wife die. You have twenty minutes."

The phone call ended with the beep of the portable. Steve looked around the large family room of the apartment. A dim light beside a beige sofa pushed away the dark from the corner of the room. The sofa was surrounded by wood furniture and encased by maroon walls the colour of dark blood. Steve told both mother and son to sit on either side of the couch.

Before I let the kid go, I asked Steve, "You know this one?"

"Came around the bar the other day."

It fit: Tommy was introducing his boy to the family business. The kid had been given a low-level muscle job to toughen him, the way his old man had probably been toughened. The kid tried to deal with Steve and came out with the short end of the stick and a swollen head. Steve had made an impact that no one could miss. The kid's face was like a billboard broadcasting the boy's ineptitude to everyone. The billboard caught Tommy's eye, and turned it to Steve and Sandra. The kid fouled up, and dear old dad was stepping in to show junior how to handle a tough situation. I grabbed the kid by the belt and heaved him to the couch. He had to use his hands to prevent himself from crashing into his mother. Once they were seated together on the couch, the rage began.

"You're dead, you animal. My husband is going to find you and your family, you greasy shit. You and him." The word "animal" betrayed her heritage; it came out as if there was an "eh" on the end of the word that wasn't there when I said it.

The son stared at me, burning holes in my chest, saying nothing. I leaned against a wall and watched Steve. This was Steve without Sandra. She could calm him down. She could reason with him. By taking her, Talarese had taken reason and restraint away from Steve. There was no one to stop him. No one to try to calm him down. It was like taking the bars off the zoo. The wild was loose in the city, and everywhere there was prey. He set the wicker chair beside Tommy's mother upright, placing it over her body, and sat in it. Her head protruded between his feet and he sat staring down into her open eyes. The curses kept coming from Maria, hurling at Steve like javelins meant to pierce his soul.

He stared at the dead woman between the legs of the chair and interrupted Maria. "You know what your husband is?"

"Oh, I know, and you're going to find out exactly what he is. You just wait. Just wait!"

Steve looked at Maria. Their hatred fought each other in stares. Neither looked away; not even Steve as he raised the gun in his hand and wordlessly shot Maria in the knee.

As the two living family members huddled in agony, Steve went to the kitchen and grabbed a towel. He threw it at the son and told him to tie it around his mother's wounded leg. I stayed true to my word and did not interfere.

The gunshot had made the room quiet for ten minutes until a mechanical buzzing turned Steve's attention away from the two on the couch. Steve opened his phone and spoke. "Are you okay? . . . I know . . . It'll be okay now. Is he with you? Tell him to come home . . . It will be fine, I promise . . . I love you, too. Tell him to come home now." Steve disconnected and closed the phone. He had not let Sandra try to calm him down; he wasn't going back to his cage until he was done.

Ten minutes after that quiet conversation, the door opened. Tommy walked in, swearing at Steve about the nerve he had and where they would find his body. If he was fearful of two men holding his family hostage at gunpoint, he didn't show it. He moved across the room quickly like an overzealous prizefighter. He was so brazen that he walked past me without giving me a second thought as he continued his verbal barrage at Steve. Steve nodded to me, and I hooked Tommy hard in the right kidney. The punch drove all the air out of his lungs with a grunt that made the second hook, to the left side, only as audible as the dull thud of my fist against his soft flesh. He crumpled to the floor without another word.

When he raised his head he saw his family as if for the first time. "Maria, what happened? Look at the blood . . . Oh, my God, Ma!"

He got off the carpet and ran to the couch to embrace his family. They sobbed together, holding each other tight. It was almost touching if you could forget why they were together on the couch. After a while Tommy pulled himself away from the embrace and stared at his mother for a long moment, then at Steve, and finally at me.

"You two fucks are dead. Dead!"

Steve raised the gun and spoke softly. "Is she back alone?"

Tommy screamed, "I'm going to kill you myself, you dirty prick. You, then that bitch of yours. Then I'm gonna burn that shithole down!"

Steve pointed the gun at Maria's other knee. "Tommy!" she shrieked. "Tell him please. I want him to leave. Please . . . tell him!"

She again broke into wordless cries and moans. Tommy stared at his wife for at least ten seconds. With each passing second his shoulders shook more and more. He finally erupted. "Shut up! Shut up!" he shouted at his wife. "Do you know who I am? Do you? Huh? No one does this to me! I made my bones. I'm made, and this piece of shit thinks he can do this? He's dead!"

"Tommy please . . . I . . . I need a hospital."

Tommy slapped his wife with a closed fist. She was trying to make him show that he cared, to make him show weakness. Tommy would never show weakness in front of us — it wasn't in him. Even with his back against the wall, he would never let anyone see under the hard skin he wore like armour. He hit her again and again until his son tried to intervene. Tommy didn't stop; his fists found the boy too. Both mother and son gave up and accepted their lumps. Tommy hit them both until he was breathing in heavy gasps. He turned to look at us once again and seemed to regain his composure. It was no wonder he was a made man and not just some strong-arm; he was trying to control the situation. He was trying to pass the events off like something that could never hurt him. Tommy was trying to show us that he was unafraid, and that it was us who should have been terrified regardless of the gun we held. He looked at us in disbelief, a look that told us we had made the biggest mistake of our lives. His look told us we should run and hide to avoid the fury of this self-proclaimed mob god. Tommy could have pulled it off too if we weren't who we were. He had no idea that there were others just as ruthless as he was. Other people who were capable of handling their own affairs instead of just passing them off to the many arms of the underworld.

Steve sighed and shot Tommy in the shoulder. The bullet hit him high on the right side of his body and spun him around, and down onto all fours. When he tried to get up, Steve kicked him hard in the ribs. Tommy flopped to his side, propelled by the foot and the crunching sound of his ribs. Steve stepped on the bullet wound and over the screams asked a third time.

"Is she back alone?"

"Yah, she's back alone. She's alone. Okay?"

Steve looked to me and said, "Check."

I went over to him, took the phone from his pocket, hit redial, and waited. When Sandra answered, I had her check outside for cars and men. She told me the streets were empty. I told her to lock up and stay put, then I told Steve everything was good. He nodded and looked around the room. The fire in him seemed to slowly drain. He looked at me, and there was less anger and violence in his eyes.

"Is there any way out of this?"

Steve knew the mob wouldn't forget, and that they would keep coming until they were satisfied. Satisfaction would most likely involve the death of Steve, Sandra, and probably me. I had been working for Paolo Donati almost exclusively for a few years, and he owed me some favours. Unfortunately, favours from a mob boss are like Grandma's china — nice to have, but you never thought of actually using it.

"I'll do what I can."

The gun sounded three more times, and we were on our way out. I had Steve wipe everything he had touched before we closed the door. In the lobby, the doorman was still on the floor and the streets were still clear. I wasn't worried about the gunshots. I figured the neighbours knew who Talarese was and what he was into. That made them the type of people who would turn up the television to drown out gunshots rather than call nine-one-one.

I drove Steve back to the bar and let him out in front of the entrance. He rode back without saying a word and got out the same way. He began to walk away, but stopped and turned to stare at me. He came back to the car and sat in the seat beside me again. He looked like hell; his shirt was bloodstained, and his pants were dirty.

"I don't know why," he said, looking at me.

I stared out the windshield and thought about why. Why had I put it all on the line for a bartender and his wife? I wasn't one of the good guys. I was on the other side. Steve came to see me because he knew I would know who took his wife. But even though I knew the men who kidnapped Sandra, I never considered myself like them. There was a line separating what I was from what they were. I was independent; I chose the jobs I wanted to work. It just so happened that one person in particular used me for my skills more than others. Paolo recognized my usefulness early on and he used me for jobs that required the ignorance and secrecy that only an outsider could provide. I worked on the fringe and I made Paolo aware of where everyone stood, be they gangs, other organized outfits, even cops. Being an outsider, I couldn't use information I found to hurt Paolo: no one would talk to me or believe what I said. There were also the hoods he employed who would have been happy to kill me for no other reason than to relieve their boredom. I lived the life I was taught. I was off the grid to everyone. No one knew where I lived; I had no accounts or property in my name. I hardly had a name — just the one word I used for an identity. I was a ghost in the machine. No one saw me coming and no one traced me back to anyone.

I stared out the window, thinking of the why, unable to find an answer. "Go see her," was all I said.

Steve nodded and grunted something as he got out of the car again. Sandra opened the door as he walked away from me and ran outside to him. They hugged in the street and cried together, two people who refused to follow the rules. I sat for a time watching the two forms joined together with arms and lips. I smiled and found myself thinking of my parents. All the years I had lived with my uncle had never shown me what they were. I learned what they did, but I never knew who they were. No matter how hard I tried to climb into their world, they were unknown. I could only hold on to their memories like the edges of dreams. I had parts and images, but no real recollection of them. I thought of them as I watched Steve and Sandra in the rain. I saw two people who fought the system to make their own life. Two people who went outside the rules to protect their small family. In that moment I felt closer to my parents, closer to two people who fought to give me a life I had no right to have as the son of bandits. Steve and Sandra refused to give in to the mob, refused to give in to their filthy pressure. They wanted a life on their terms, and I helped them get that — maybe only for a short time longer.

I pulled away from the curb and drove to a coffee shop around the corner. I found a spot behind it and parked, then sat in the car watching the streetlights fade into large blotches in the growing fog on the windshield. I got myself involved in a mess, and getting out was not going to be easy. I needed to meet with the boss before word got out — or worse, a contract.

I got out of the car into the glow of the streetlight and walked to the coffee shop to the beat of the gravel under my shoes. I used the storefront windows to check out everyone in the shop before making a move to enter. No one looked out at me. No one even looked in the direction of the doors. I moved through the pair of doors separating outside from inside and ordered a tea at the counter. I sat at a table for two against the wall and watched everything that was going on in the restaurant. The counter had stools lined up for solitary eaters at a red scarred countertop. Sugar, napkins, and ketchup were the only decorations in

MIKE KNOWLES

the restaurant. Four men sat in the red swivel stools at the counter and ate in silence. One waitress served them in her T-shirt and apron. She didn't move fast and she didn't move slow; she did her job with quiet efficiency amid the hum of the air conditioner and the clanging that sporadically erupted from the kitchen behind her.

The waitress came out from behind the counter and brought me my tea. After she had left me the water, a mug, and a metal container full of milk, I thought over the events of the day. I had witnessed the deaths of seven people who were connected in their own right. I hadn't killed anyone, but I hadn't stopped the killing either, so I was as guilty as Steve. If I didn't try to square this away, Steve and Sandra would be dead by tomorrow, and I would follow soon after. Steve wouldn't give me up, but they would make it hard on Sandra and she would — in the end. I had to try to mop this up before it spilled over into the streets.

I drank my tea slowly and turned a quarter in my hand. The only way it was going to work was if I had a sit-down with the boss himself to give an explanation. Tommy had kidnapped and threatened to mutilate Steve's wife for overdue rent. He went outside the natural order of things, and it had cost him. If someone doesn't pay up you beat them, or burn their place down. People don't pay when they're dead. Dead bodies also have the bad habit of attracting cops; no one wants cops. I had to make Paolo see it this way because the only other way to see it was two men decided they wanted to die in the worst possible way, so they picked a fight with a made man and his family. I finished the tea and left a few bucks on the table, then walked to the phone and dialled.

"Yeah?"

"It's Wilson. I need a meeting with the man."

"I'm sorry, sir, I think you have the wrong —"

"I'm coming now and I'll wait. Pass on a message that I have something important to speak to him about."

"You can't —"

I hung up the phone before the lackey could finish and made my way to the counter. I sat among the silent men and had another tea and a muffin to make myself busy for ten more minutes.

I finished eating, paid up, and drove. I got out of the car four blocks from the restaurant and walked the rest of the way. I wanted everyone to see me coming.

There were always four men out front discussing sports, food, or the women who walked by. The group changed members every couple of hours, but their purpose never changed. They were the first level of security, and if they didn't like the look of you, you weren't going anywhere. I crossed the street directly across from the front entrance and watched as the group of four men seamlessly shifted to block my way. By the time I stepped up onto the curb, I was on a collision course with the group as though that was my intention all along. The one to my left spoke as the others closed in around me.

"You got balls, Wilson, showing up like you call the shots."

I didn't answer because it was meant as a statement, not a challenge. One of the men to my right, shielded from view by his partners, began frisking me. It was a waste of time, I was clean; I left the gun in my car. When the frisk ended I was still in the middle. No one moved.

"I'm going in now, anything stupid and you're going to get hurt first," I said to the one who had spoken. He stared at me, and I let my face pull into a grin. It wasn't productive to do this, but I always hated being frisked. Even more, I hated being stalled by four idiots in a lame attempt at intimidation once I had been found to be unarmed. I brushed past the man to my left, making sure to edge him hard. I never turned back, not even when the four began hurling insults at me.

Inside the door it was immediately dimmer. On my right was a young woman behind a mahogany counter — another layer of security. The coat-check girl checked over whoever came in and called ahead with any problems.

"Check your coat, sir?"

"Maybe later," I said as I walked past the coat-check girl to a set of thick glass doors that led to the dining room.

"Everyone checks their coats, sir, house rules." Her voice had a hard edge to it; the word "sir" sounded as though it meant "you dumb asshole." I turned to the voice with my hand on one of the cold glass doors. She was short, maybe five feet, with long dark hair and eyes that matched. She was cute, not pretty, and that fact probably gave her a lot of attitude under her exterior. Knowing she would never be considered beautiful hardened her. She wasn't really cute at that moment because she was doing her best to give me a hard stare.

"I know what everyone does, and I don't care." The look in my eyes cut through her stare and for a split second she was scared. Her left hand moved under the counter — just an inch.

"If you're thinking of moving that left hand a little more, you should think of one thing first," I said.

She paused, wondering what I knew that she didn't. "What's that?" Her voice had no edge now, just a hesitant fear.

"I'll be through the door before you can get your hand above the counter." I never knew what she did once the door closed behind me.

The lights in the dining room were dim; they made the red walls a dark maroon. There were twenty tables below the five stairs in front of me. Past the tables was a hallway; on either side of the hall were booths. I walked down the stairs past the tables, each of which had a long tablecloth and four overturned chairs on top. Once I made my way past the tables, two men from booths on opposite sides of the mouth of the hall stood and approached me.

"Stay where you are."

I stood my ground. I could see that the two men in front of me had guns in shoulder holsters under their suit jackets. On top of that, the bodyguards were young and in shape. These two were first-rate newbies, immature and eager, like all before them. They must have had long and bloody résumés already, to be doing personal security for the boss.

"Turn around. Arms straight out."

I did as I was told and stared at the wall. The frisk was by the numbers, and more thorough than outside because this frisk was less about weapons and more about a wire. As by-the-books as it was, it was a slow job, something that didn't sit right with me. Too much time was spent on my upper body and arms. These guys were young, but they should have been good because the position they were in demanded skill. I kept thinking they should have been better than this. As a right hand moved slowly down my left leg, I realized what was happening, and my world exploded.

One moment I was standing, thinking only of the meeting and the frisking; the next I was on the floor forcing myself to breath as I tried to focus and forget that one of my kidneys just exploded. I lay sprawling for thirty seconds and then I managed to roll onto my back.

I saw Julian outlined by the light. His bulk was like the moon eclipsing the sun. All at once, he was massive and terrifying. He was made more so by the fact that I was laying at his feet viewing him only in quick flashes as I spasmed on the floor.

"You got a mouth on you. You talk too much. Always saying something. See what your mouth gets you. You get hurt. Maybe you get killed."

My mouth moved but nothing came out. A hard voice, cultured by years of smoke, alcohol, and acid reflux spoke out. "Get him over here."

At once Julian stooped and lifted me over a shoulder. I sloshed around watching the world reel. Inside me the anger was boiling, and for a moment I forgot why I had come. I should have been humble, quiet, and polite, but the rage pounding in my ears erased thoughts and rationality. My body was hanging so that I was chest to chest with the monster of a man. Despite the pain, I straightened my body so that Julian looked to be carrying a load of lumber on his shoulder. The pain in my back hit me and I almost buckled, but I managed to stay horizontal. I drove my elbow back hard, aiming at Julian's eye. He saw the blow coming, shrugged his shoulders, and tried to drop me. My elbow connected with his cheekbone before I was airborne

I landed behind Julian, on all fours, and saw that he had covered his face and turned away. I covered the distance between us in three steps and kicked him hard in the groin like I was going for a field goal. Julian dropped to his knees, and I kept coming. The next two kicks hit the back of his neck and knocked him down. The three stomps to the groin that followed should have kept him there, but he pulled in his knees and got up. He stood and smoothly extracted a large revolver from under his suit coat. I knew from the small distance between us that I was dead. No diving could get me out of range. I stared at him, but no bullet came. Julian waited. Even though he had me cold, he waited. He wanted the order, and it hadn't come yet. I knew right there that the monster in front of me would be a force soon. He didn't lose his head. As mad as he was, he followed protocol. I waited for a thirty-second year as the gun stared at me without flinching.

"Heh, he's like a dog, Wilson. You get into his yard, and he wants to fuck you to show you he's on top. Down boy. Let him sit."

Paolo was behind Julian in a booth — invisible beyond Julian's massive frame and his gun.

"I said sit!"

The gun didn't move, so I did. I walked around Julian and sat in a chair facing the lone man in the booth. Paolo was comfortable in the smoky dim light. He wore a tailored grey suit and tie, but he didn't look professional. The lines, the scars, and the ugliness in his face told his real credentials.

"You have nerve to tell me you're coming here. Like I need to wait on you, like you're somebody. This information better be important, boy."

I did the only thing I could do. I told him what had transpired. During my quiet retelling his face never moved. Only his eyes gave away his feelings. His eyes blazed, and his pupils violently shook. His expressionless face held eyes that forced out an anger that could not be articulated. Out of the corner of my eye, out of earshot, Julian stood smirking. He saw the eyes and knew the order would come. He was happy to be the hand of those raging eyes.

I didn't mince words. I told Paolo everything, but I never explained why I got involved; it would have violated every rule I was ever taught in my second education. My reasons were my own, and I wasn't sharing them with the burning eyes across from me. Paolo knew nothing of my life before I met him, and I kept it that way. I would never give him the ability to understand any part of me. Any understanding could lead to leverage. I focused on Tommy and the line he crossed to be a role model to his boy. Hassling, strong-arming, and threats were part of life here, but it never escalated to what Tommy had done. Every taboo was broken for money in Hamilton, but some rules had to hold so that anarchy didn't erupt. More important, the rules we had separated us from other organizations more than colours or territory ever could. Organizations from different parts of the globe who settled in the city didn't place any importance on rules. They wanted power and they were willing to push anyone to get it. Paolo and his crew looked down on the new gangs and their methods. Paolo's men saw themselves not as thugs and hoods, but as professionals in a business that had employed generations of families. Everyone who did business outside the law in a different manner was deemed inferior because they ignored the methods established over the years by true career criminals.

The story ended with silence. I stopped talking and stared straight at Paolo Donati. I didn't beg for mercy or plead for understanding. I told him part of what I wanted to say and I waited for the verdict.

"Rules," he said. "Fucking rules. You have got to be kidding me. We kill people all the time, with guns, knives, shit they force through holes into their bodies. Hell, we even put whores on the streets. Everything we do hurts everybody, and you want to tell me there are rules now?"

"There's always been rules. Some people forget them, but I don't. What Tommy did was out of line."

"Don't you say his name. He was family, you fuck. Family! You get that? And you, you're like some ungrateful stepchild. You get paid by me. What I do, what Tommy did, made the money you earn. And you have the balls to come to me and tell me you're following rules. Fuck your rules."

His hand stamped the end of his sentence into the table. I was less worried. Yelling meant the situation was not cut and dried. If he wanted me dead, it would have been done already. The yelling made me think he knew the other half of what I wanted to say. My thoughts drowned out his rage until one sentence brought me back.

"Leave us alone."

Everyone, even Julian, slowly moved away, leaving Paolo and me completely isolated. "Why did you do it? And don't bullshit me with that rules crap. I know you don't believe in that shit."

"There are rules . . ."

"Bullshit!" he roared.

I took a second and considered the man who held my fate in his breath. "My reasons are my own. Now, do you want to hear the rest?"

The old man leaned back, his eyes dulled a fraction, and I almost saw a smile. "Tell me," he said.

"Tommy was more trouble than he was worth. All the brutality with the Russians cost you. He was so over the top that they banded together to fight him. He unified them, made them stronger. He's the reason you didn't take the Russians out. All his bloodshed brought public attention down on you. For a while there Tommy's work was regular in the newspapers. There had to be a truce."

I paused to see if he was listening. "Talk," he said.

"Now you have to live side by side with the Russians. You have lines between them and you. Tommy was the guard on your side. He was a reminder of how bad things could be again. Tommy was a guard dog, but he was always behind a fence. You never let him out to work anywhere else because you knew how destructive his presence could be. Now Tommy is dead, and so is his family."

"So how does your treason help me?"

"It's an act of war."

"You're right about that. You put a stick in a hornet's nest, and for what? Some greasy mick? This war will swallow you up."

"Not if I'm not the one blamed. If word got out that the Russians killed Tommy, you would have a reason to take back all the Russians have. You can do it right this time, without Tommy to screw it up. He'd be more useful in death than in life. He'll be a symbol now. He'll be the why. His death gives you a reason to break the truce. You couldn't pull him off the wall before; it would have shown you didn't trust him. That he was wrong. You can't show that kind of weakness to the Russians."

"Why would I want to go up against the Russians again?"

"They're into things you aren't, and they've already set up a system people are used to. All you have to do is slide in and take over everything they started." It was true, the Russians had come to town slowly, starting with the local hockey team. The team brought over two Russians to add speed to their second line. The players were given fancy cars as signing bonuses and were paid a good salary. Almost at once, the locals back home kidnapped the players' parents for ransom. After a successful payoff, the boys back home got better ideas. They blackmailed the players into using their contacts with the hockey team to ask for visas for key members of Russian organized crime. Once they were given access to the country, the mobsters set up companies using the hockey stars' names to garner capital and investors. These companies were fronts for gathering more work visas, and for money laundering. In time, we had our own Russian mafia cell in the city. The hockey team had brought speed to the team and even more corruption to the city.

The Russian neighbourhoods were reintroduced to the corruption they left behind in the motherland. The poor Russian immigrants had a hard-wired distrust for authority, and simply slipped back into the pattern of paying for protection. The gangsters called the protection *"krysha,"* which means "roof." The people who paid were under the protection of a criminal roof — and everyone paid. It wasn't only money that was extorted; the gangsters had been known to become part owners of businesses, or the pro-bono clients of high-paid attorneys. The Russian mob was growing and soon it would branch out again.

"Crows eat their own. Did you know that?" Paolo changed the direction of the conversation at once.

"No, I didn't."

"Not all crows, but it has been shown that crows have been known to eat eggs and other chicks."

I said nothing, so Paolo continued. "The crows don't do this for enjoyment. No, far from it. They eat other crows' eggs so that their own eggs have a better chance to survive. They're cannibals. See, those birds kill their own for survival. That is a society without rules. That is a society where anarchy exists. That is the society you want to fucking bring to my doorstep. You want me to watch you eat my fucking family, my people, like I was a crow. I am no bird, you crow. I am the king of this fucking jungle." His hands gripped the table so tightly his knuckles were white with the strain.

"You aren't a crow," I said. "But Tommy is dead, and there is no changing it. You kill me and Steve and you get revenge, but then your symbol will be gone and forgotten. How long before the Russians come over the line? With the butcher dead, they will move out to your territory. Do you want that kind of message? People will ask who it was the Russians were afraid of. Was it you or Tommy? And soon in the back alleys and bars people will say, 'This never would have happened if Tommy was alive.' When that happens your teeth won't look so sharp anymore, and you'll have to fight your own people while the Russians watch."

Paolo said nothing; he just stared at me. His knuckles on the edge of the table were still white with strain. Slowly the white faded pink as the hands relaxed and the blood returned. "Listen up, crow. You're done with me. Out of business. I don't want to see you again. I'm not going to kill you yet. You've been loyal — more than Tommy, and that's something, since you aren't family like he is . . . he was." The boss let out a low laugh that ended in a small cough. "Ironic, isn't it? You're getting saved by loyalty."

"The business with the bar . . . is it finished then?" I asked politely.

"You got some nerve asking about a shithole bar like that. One word out of my mouth, just one, and I'd blow that bar down like the big bad fucking wolf."

"I know it and I understand, but I need to know if it's done."

"Caw, caw, little bird. You don't need to know shit. What I do is none of your business. None. Julian." With that one word the massive human frame just out of earshot came to life and moved towards me. I stood before he could get next to me.

I walked out past Julian. Neither of us said a word to the other, but I could feel the violence inside me slamming against the side of my skull. I winked at the coat-check girl at the entrance who eyed me, as I passed, with her hand under the counter. The four protectors out front gave a low whistle when I came through the doors. They were surprised to see me leaving under my own power. If they ever found out what I had told Paolo, they would hate themselves forever for not shooting me down when they had the chance. That was the difference between most people involved in the mob and Paolo. Paolo wasn't ruled by his emotions; he was cold, calculating, and educated. I had put together pieces of who Paolo Donati was from information I learned on the street. His father was the top of the totem pole before him, and he sent his kids to the best schools. Paolo grew up in the best neighbourhood, next to doctors and millionaires, and went to school with the other neighbourhood rich kids. Paolo's upbringing couldn't have been more different from his father's. He didn't have to fight and hustle every day to survive. Paolo had friends, girlfriends, and good grades. He excelled in math and science. People say he was studying to be a veterinarian, but that is probably bullshit invented because Paolo loved to talk about animals. He used them as metaphors to degrade a person. He spoke of the nature of the animal kingdom to show people how close they were to those lower on the food chain. Paolo never did anything with his science and math, except use it to intimidate. His schooling ended abruptly when he was called to the family business at twenty-three. There he encountered animals, but they weren't the kind in books. These animals were much worse, and in time Paolo ruled them all.

Paolo studied people as if they were locked in at the zoo; he analyzed details and missed very little. Nothing I had told him was a new idea to him. He understood Tommy, his behaviour, and the delicate balance his presence maintained. Paolo saw his empire as a vast ecosystem, and he would not allow it to become unbalanced. Unbalance meant he was not in control, and that chaos signalled weakness. For someone who thrived on being in control, being the king of his jungle as he put it, weakness was worse than death. If things were to spin out of control, Paolo would want to be the one doing the spinning.

MIKE KNOWLES

I walked the four blocks, alone, back to the car. I drove, listening to the Volvo as it accelerated through its gears. I was forever connected to a maniac and his girl in the murder of seven people, and I was out of a job. I had pushed a group of very dangerous people toward another group of very dangerous people. There would be bloodshed for what I had done. I tried to console myself with the idea that war with the Russians was inevitable, and that the fight would be over quickly with the Italians rallying around the memory of Tommy Talarese. But I was wrong.

Paolo began a war with the Russians that raged for years. More lines were drawn, and the city became more divided than ever. I was wrong about being out of a job, too. I was working again less than a month later.

# CHAPTER SEVEN

The dashboard clock read 4:23 as I slowed on the street where the Volvo was parked. Steve got out and told me he'd meet me back at the bar. I rolled Steve's Range Rover down the street and watched 22 Hess out of the corner of my eye. There weren't any squad cars yet, so Steve was good to go. I used the cell phone Steve left on the seat to call him.

"It's all clear," I said.

"I can see that. Let's meet at the bar."

Back at Sully's Tavern I ordered a Coke and waited for Steve. I made small talk with Ben and Sandra and went over the events of the day in my head. I showed up at 22 Hess to find out about what I stole from the airport and to figure out how to get those amateurs off my ass. The computer nerds stole accounting information from someone working for what looked to be the Russian mob. They blackmailed the accountant and set up an exchange at the airport. When the airport exchange didn't happen the accountant likely had to 'fess up to his employers about what was going on. The Russians had their own way of dealing with blackmailers that didn't involve airport hand-offs. They came looking for the geeks and their property at the same time I did. So now I was in a Mexican stand-off, with two big guns pointed at my head.

The first gun was in Paolo's hand. According to the dingy Guinness clock on the wall, I had just over a day and a half to get everything in order before Paolo decided to cut his losses. If I were viewed as a liability when Julian returned to see me, Paolo would turn him loose on me in an effort to keep himself insulated from the airport job.

The second gun belonged to the Russians. They were after their property and they had no problem killing a whole office staff to get closer to what they wanted. The Russians were real thugs, not amateurs, and they probably had my scent because Mike had not been dead when I left the office. They would gladly grind what they needed out of me to get to what had been taken from them.

I decided that when Steve brought the car back, I would go to the office. It was the only option. There I had a chance to pick up someone doing surveillance, or wait for the Russians to find me. I would be next on the Russians' list and I had no way of finding them without drawing attention to myself. There was no way the Italians would help me. Paolo had no interest in helping me when it was just the amateurs who were following me. There was no way he would help me deal with the Russians. I had to play defence — alone.

Steve pulled in twenty minutes after my second Coke and tossed the car keys at me as he walked to Sandra. He kissed her on the cheek and asked her questions in low tones. They both smiled and talked for two and a half minutes while Ben tended bar; no one complained about how slow service had suddenly gotten. When Steve finished talking to Sandra, he kissed her on the cheek and came over to me. He leaned in, resting his knotted forearms on the bar.

"They had guys at the corners scanning the cars," he told me.

"I never saw them," I said.

"They were around the streets. I saw one stop what he was doing to stare at me getting in the car. I guess I was okay in their eyes 'cause no one tailed me."

"You sure?" I asked.

"Yep," was the only response I got.

I told Steve I'd see him later and left the bar to make my way to the office. I found the car on a side street. It hummed to life without any problems, and the tank was full. I smiled at my friend's wordless act of kindness. As I drove, I tried to clear my head of all the thoughts I was having. I couldn't be afraid or hesitate. I had to walk head up into a trap and make it work to my advantage. This was the opposite of everything I wanted, everything I was trained to do. The situation also had no real plan to go along with it. I always planned everything or at least had an idea about how I wanted to spin a situation. I remembered the words of my uncle: "Planning separates the living and the dead, boy. Don't forget it. The morgue is full of guys who thought they could handle anything." I knew that deep down he was talking about my parents; they didn't have a good plan and in his eyes and it killed them. The events of the past few days had left me without any control, and it pissed me off. I was struggling to keep ahead of people who all seemed to know more than I did about what I was involved in.

As I drove, I breathed deep and counted down from ten until my mind was empty. I turned off Duke Street onto James Street and circled the office a few times. I let my mind take in the area, waiting for recognition of anything that stood out. I didn't see people loitering in the shadows, and there were no strange parked cars concealing occupants hunched low in their driver seats. To be safe, I went up a block and parked on a side street. I turned off the ignition and checked the Glock. I reloaded the gun so that I had eleven in the clip and one in the chamber. I took off the safety and tucked the gun into the holster at the small of my back. I made sure my shirt was out over the holster, and got out of the car.

I didn't enter the building at first. I was bait, but I planned on surviving my predators. I wanted the Russians to take a run at me on my terms, in a place where I had control. That meant I had to make it past the front door and anyone waiting. I walked on the opposite side of the street, past the office, into a variety store five doors down from my building. It was the best spot I had to watch the street. I bought a paper and a coffee and walked over to the video wall by the door. I stared over the video rack of soft- and hard-core pornography through the window to the street. I spent twenty minutes sipping my coffee and pretending to split my time between the paper and the porn.

I left after the clerk started to cough a little louder than he needed to over and over again. I hadn't noticed a thing yet, but it had been less than half an hour — nothing in the grand scheme of things. I walked back up the street and used an alley to cross over James Street, the second-busiest street in the area. I hailed a cab and gave the cabbie a story about a cheating wife. I told the driver to cruise the area so I could catch her in the act. I told him I would pay whatever the fare came to, and settled in to watch the neighbourhood roll by. The cabbie spoke about his own cheating wife and how much he hated the bitch and *her* kids. I ignored the story, speaking up only to tell him where to turn. I watched the cars and the people as we cruised; I was looking for solitary figures sitting low in car seats, or random pedestrians who strode the sidewalks too long. In the hour I spent in the cab I saw no human forms in the shadows of cars or alleys. I paid up the cabbie when we ended up back on James Street for the twelfth time, and walked the streets again.

I carefully navigated the side streets and narrow alleys. The reek of garbage from the corners accented the putrid fumes being spewed by the sewers. I walked past the convenience store I had been in earlier, then I went past the office. No one looked at me twice, and no one stood out — yet. I knew deep down that Mike had squealed on me back at the office. People were coming.

After a few more strolls around the area, I went up the steps to the building. It was almost six, after office hours; the few other rented office spaces in the building were empty. I had the key ready, and I opened the locked door and entered the building without losing a step. No one shot me in the back; no one was waiting for me inside. I moved down the hall past the elevator and entered the stairwell. I closed the door quietly behind me and waited. I waited for three minutes, listening to the hum of the fluorescent bulbs. I strained to hear any other noises above me, but there were none.

Before I started climbing the stairs, I took off my shoes. I held them in my left hand with my thumb and forefinger; my right was on the butt of my gun. Quietly I climbed the stairs. At first, my damp feet made quiet suction sounds, but the noise faded as my soles absorbed the grime and grease of the stairs. I passed each floor until I ran out of stairs at the sixth floor. No one was waiting for me on the top floor. I leaned over the stairwell and saw nothing below me, so I moved back down one flight to the fifth floor — my floor. Slowly I pressed the thumb latch on the door handle using the hand that was carrying the shoes. The first attempt was a little unsteady, so I put down the shoes and tried again. I opened the stairwell door and spied the dimly lit hallway for two minutes. Every office was dark, including mine. I didn't hear a single cough or shuffle of feet.

I picked up my shoes and moved down the hallway, making sure to stay low under each door so no one could shoot me in the back from a hiding place in one of the dark offices. I knelt to the right of my door and silently slid my key in. I turned the key, and slowly pushed the door open. I knew the score right away. The door moved too quickly; it moved open on its own and slammed against the door jamb because inside a window was open.

Behind my desk the blinds were up and the window was open. I kept low to the floor as I moved inside. Keeping the desk between me and the window, I pivoted to the blinds and released them. I didn't think anyone would shoot through the window at me; they would first want to find out what I knew. I was sure I had about two minutes until whoever was watching the window would be at the office door, so I got ready quick. I put my shoes on and went to the closet. The closet had a false back. I pulled out the painted wood piece that sat behind my clothes and took out a modified double-barrelled shotgun that I had sawn down to twelve inches. The shotgun was useless outside of ten feet, but up close it was like the wrath of God — scarring everything in its path. I stood, gun in hand, to the right of the door — out of the line of fire from both the hall and the window.

I was off on the time. The door was kicked open after five minutes. The bull who hit the door was a middle-aged guy with a beard, a beer belly, and scars around his eyes.

He used a shoulder to hit the door, leaving his gun pointed at the floor. The grey suit he wore pulled at the buttons under the strain of his gut. He must have weighed two hundred forty pounds; most of it was flab. The crash through the door brought him into the room three feet from the shotgun.

I stayed where I was and waited for the man to catch sight of me out of the corner of his eye. His head turned to mine, and I watched the realization hit his face. I saw it in almost slow motion. Each muscle twitched, turning his face into a look of shock. He didn't say a word, and he didn't move; he just stood in front of me. We looked at each other for a quarter of a minute until a voice came from the hall.

"Gregor?"

The Russians had found me. I didn't speak because I wasn't sure I would be understood. I motioned down with the shotgun and waited. Gregor put his gun down and lowered himself to his knees. I moved his gun to me with my foot, never letting the shotgun drift from Gregor's centre. The voice called again, more sternly; it had the severity of a man in charge. I butted Gregor on the side of the face, and he went down the rest of the way to the floor. The noise was a sick wet bump, and the groan from Gregor's lips brought the hallway man into the room with his gun drawn.

As the welt on Gregor's temple grew, the second Russian and I waited with guns pointed at each other. I broke the silence. "You want to sit down?"

A heavily accented voice returned my pleasant invitation. "Not with guns drawn."

I'd had enough shit for one day. "Put yours down and we can talk — if you don't I'm going to do some terrible things."

I planted my feet and got ready. I began counting down

from ten in my head. At one, I was going to kill him and risk the consequences. I figured the risk to be low: the shotgun blast would push him back and draw his shot wide. That was, of course, unless he was counting in his head too — with a lower number than mine. At four, he agreed to sit. He tucked his shiny gun into his pants and sat in the chair next to Gregor's body. I sat behind my desk and set the shotgun on the desk, the barrel pointed towards the Russian and Gregor.

"Now what do you and Gregor want?" I asked.

The second Russian was the new face of the mob: in his twenties, fresh-faced, dyed hair, gym membership. The new breed of mobster was unlike any of its predecessors. They were into their work for more than money, they were into it for a sense of identity. The lack of a war to fight in left many kids looking for a cause, and the mob was more than willing to let them enlist. These recruits served with a vicious devotion that would scare Germans from the forties. What these kids lacked in skill they more than made up for with brutality.

"Uh . . . money."

"You already snuck in once and left the window open. You went through my shit too. You tried to make it look like you didn't, but I can see that things are out of place, so don't bullshit me with some story about a robbery. You were here looking for something and you didn't find it. You waited for me to come back so you could ask me some hard questions. Once you got your answers, you were going to kill me. I want to know why. Who are you working for? And what do they want with me?"

He took a few seconds before he answered. "I do not know what you are speaking about. Now please, call police."

He looked unafraid of the prospect of involving the

police. Handcuffs were better than death, and he knew deep down that I wasn't the type of person who would call the cops. He started to smile, probably thinking I would let him go. I felt my face pull to the left and I grinned at his smile. His eyes lost their mirth and his mouth formed a small, confused O. His gaze drifted down to the shotgun on the table, then back to me, and then again to the gun. He sprang from his chair, like he was shot out of a cannon, and grabbed at the barrel of the gun. He was lifting the shotgun off the desk when my hand came out from behind my back with the Glock. My grin didn't fade when I shot him.

The bullet hit him in the shoulder and put him on the ground. The bang was loud, but the offices were empty. No one would complain about the noise. I got out of the chair and moved around the desk. The sound of the shot had woken Gregor. He didn't make a sound when I kicked him in the temple; he just went limp and sagged to the floor again. His partner was still conscious as I picked him up off the floor. I took his fancy nickel-plated gun from his pants and pushed him over the desk so I could empty the rest of his pockets. Gum, cigarettes, a wallet, a knife, and a cell phone hit my desk in succession. I shoved the Russian back in his chair, grabbed a tea towel, and pressed it hard on the wound to get him to wake all the way up. His eyes focused, and we were back where we had started — minus a bit of his shoulder.

I sat back down behind the desk and put the Glock on the blotter. I didn't point it at him; I just let it sit casually.

"Now, what did you and Gregor want?" I asked. The edge in my voice told him I was serious. The hole in his shoulder proved it.

He stared at me, his eyes wide and shifting left to right. He was trying to think up a story.

"You've got thirty seconds to make me interested,

otherwise I'll kill you where you sit. Then I'll start talking with Gregor. Seeing you dead will more than convince him to tell me what I need to know. The way I see it, you have a choice: are you going to be more useful to me dead or alive?"

The eyes shifted wildly again like a person drowning thrashes for air. After twenty seconds, his shoulders relaxed; he was ready to feed me the split. Most people under duress give you a sixty-forty split — sixty percent bullshit, forty percent honesty. People figure it's just enough to save them but not enough to do any real harm. I picked up the gun to speed up the split.

"Okay, okay, shit," he said in a voice that gained its base speaking an eastern language.

"Name, kid, then your boss."

"My . . . my name is Igor. I work for Sergei Vidal."

"Kid, you work for whoever gives you an order. Somebody else might sign the cheques, but your real boss is the one ordering you around. Now give me a local name and stop trying to impress me."

I could tell that this wasn't where Igor wanted the conversation to go. He wanted me to be terrified of the name of his employer and leave town as fast as possible out of fear and good judgement. He didn't know that I had played the game longer and better than him. A fact that should have been evident, considering he ambushed me and he was the one who got shot.

"I don't know who is in charge, I find out through . . ."

The sentence trailed off as I picked up the gun. I was so tired of amateurs and bullshit. It was getting late in the evening, and I wanted sleep — not more work.

"Consider that strike two. No bullet for that, but strike three gets you ejected from the game. And when that happens Gregor will be the next at bat," I said in a calm matter-of-fact voice.

MIKE KNOWLES

Igor slackened in his chair while I waited patiently for the second split, the last split. "My boss . . . his name is Mikhail. He works in a private club on Barton."

"What kind of club?" I asked.

"It's a social club, for cards and drinking."

"Name of the bar, Igor. No bullshit this time."

He looked at his feet then the left wall. He was looking at it hard like it might open up so that he could dash through to safety. His eyes were glistening. The kid was realizing he wasn't going to become a powerful gangster. He now understood that, because of what he had failed to do, he would end up dead, and that it would be his friends and co-workers who were going to kill him. It's a hard realization the first time you feel it.

"It's called the Kremlin," he said in a low, quiet voice. It was the voice of a traitor.

I had a decision to make about what to do with Igor and Gregor. Killing them would be more trouble than it was worth. Disposing of bodies takes time, and it's hard to do unnoticed when you're in the heart of the city. There are too many people rushing out from each artery. Each person would bring with him complications I didn't need. Letting them go would be much easier; they were in too much trouble to stick around. They both fucked up. They didn't do their job, and they sold out their boss. They had to run far and quick before word was out.

"I'm going to the Kremlin, and I'm keeping your phone. If I find out you lied, I'm calling every number stored in the phone using your name to find out what I need to know."

Igor's eyes were glistening. He had just grown up in five minutes, and it was taking its toll fast. He already looked older, weaker.

"I'm dead then," he said.

"You're not dead yet, but you've got a hell of a head start. You better start running. Both of you. When I show up at the club, everyone will be looking for you two. So you better run fast and far."

MIKE KNOWLES

# CHAPTER EIGHT

watched Igor and Gregor help each other out of the office. I had their guns and a ruined rug. The blood on the rug was not a huge problem — in my line of work blood is a constant issue. Under the rug was a tarp cut to match its dimensions. I moved the chairs and rolled up the rug, pulling the tarp with it as a barrier. I used some duct tape to secure it and found a trash bag for the guns I took off the morons. Keeping guns is dumber than keeping a bloodstained rug. Guns have history, which can become your future for ten to twenty years if you get caught with one.

I stowed the shotgun in the closet and holstered the Glock behind my back. I also took the time to rifle through my desk for my credit cards. In the back of the drawer, stuck in the right-hand corner with a magnet, was a stack of clean credit cards and the item I was looking for.

Years ago I took a card off a small-time mugger. It looked like a platinum American Express card. In actuality it was a decorated piece of metal with a razored edge. The mugger I pulled it from used it to stick up guys in the bathrooms of bars. Once, he happened to hustle the wrong guy, and I had to remedy the situation. I took the card and used it to make sure everyone would see his face coming the next time he tried a bathroom stickup.

I pocketed the card, picked up the carpet and the guns, and walked down the darkened stairs to the basement exit. The back doors had no handle on the outside, just a push bar on the inside. I exited, listening to the click behind me as the doors resealed the building. I dragged the rug to the corner of the alley. The uneven concrete had developed craters over the years; the deeper divots in the corner were full of dark filthy water long after the rainstorms ended. I found the largest puddle and rolled the carpet in. The dirt and grime in the water soaked into the shag and added pounds of weight instantly. I towed the carpet to the nearest Dumpster and leaned it up against the side. The rug would dry black, hiding all of the stains inside, and would be on its way to the dump with the building's trash soon after that. The guns in the bag could not be taken care of so easily. I decided to use the alleys to dispose of them one piece at a time. After ten minutes, I had dismantled, wiped, and disposed of the two Russians' pistols in several sewer grates.

I had to make a stop before I visited the Kremlin. My watch read 8:33 p.m. when I opened the door to the variety store I had been in a few hours earlier. The wind chime that served as a warning bell let the clerk know I was there. He was a different man than the one who had shot me dirty looks earlier. This one was a short Middle Eastern man with close-cropped black hair. He wore the hair without gel, and its health was evident in the way it fought gravity above his scalp. His short, neatly trimmed beard framed tight lips below a large pointy nose. I didn't bother with a greeting. I moved through the aisles past jerky, corn nuts, cereal, and batteries until I finally found what I was looking for: a Trojan Magnum encased in shiny foil. I took the condom to the counter and bought it along with a pack of cigarettes, a lighter, and a lighter refill.

"Ho, ho. Big night, eh buddy?"

The smiling face across the counter beamed a conspiratorial wicked grin for three seconds, until it recognized that I wouldn't be replying. I gave him two bills and waited for my change. The clerk grumbled to himself about assholes and shitty jobs while he bagged up everything I bought. I took the bag and my change and walked out the door. The wind chime cheerily announced my departure; the angry man behind the register didn't bother with a goodbye.

I walked to the car and got in, leaving the engine off. I took out my groceries and used the plastic bag they came in as a trash bag. I tore the cellophane away from the cigarettes and opened the pack. I put a cigarette behind my ear and dumped the rest in the bag. I leaned across the passenger seat and rifled through the glove box for a Swiss Army knife I kept inside. I used the knife to work a small hole into the face of the empty cigarette pack. I tore the foil away from the Trojan and rolled the condom out. I used my finger to open the prophylactic up and then filled it tight with lighter fluid. I knotted the improvised balloon and then shoved into the cigarette package. The condom bulged at first, but I managed to work it into the confines of the empty package. I leaned across the seat and went into the glove box again. I found an old wet-nap from KFC inside, and used it to clean the condom lubrication and lighter fluid off my hands. The lemony smell of the disposable cloth erased some of the scent left by the lighter fluid. I stowed the cigarette pack in my pocket, put the remnants of what I bought in the plastic bag, and opened the car door. I got out and walked to the nearest garbage can, threw the bag in, and got back into the car. Once my pistol was stowed in the glove box, I drove to the Kremlin.

It took less than ten minutes to drive from the office to the Kremlin. Barton Street was a concrete Rolodex through the city. Every neighbourhood was connected to the street. I followed it through the Italian, Vietnamese, and Polish neighbourhoods until I found the Kremlin. I parked at the curb across the street from the club and scanned the front of the building; it was long and rectangular with a small sign that read "Private" to the left of the entryway. The door was made of heavy metal and looked like it would withstand a police battering ram. The two windows on either side of the entrance were barred with heavy black metal rods. It was clear that I wasn't getting inside the building unless I was allowed through the front door. I got out of the car and crossed the street. As I walked, I took the unlit cigarette from behind my ear and put it in my mouth, then I moved the pack of cigarettes and lighter from my pocket to my right hand. There was no doorman out front, and I expected the door to be locked. I was surprised when I pulled the door and it swung out on well-oiled hinges.

I walked inside and had to blink quickly to adjust to the lack of light. Two men in suits approached; they were similar, almost like siblings, but the resemblance wasn't genetic — it was in the scars they carried. Their noses were flat, their eyes had an abundance of scar tissue, and their ears were cauliflowered. My eyes became used to the dark enough for me to see two bulges under their suits; they had guns — big guns.

The man on the left greeted me coldly with a deep, accented voice. "I'm sorry, sir, this is a private club. You must be leaving."

His arm laced mine as the other man stepped behind me on my right. I didn't move. "Tell Mikhail there's someone here with business to discuss."

"You will be leaving now." The voice didn't rise in volume; it just mechanically repeated its command.

"Listen, I'm not moving. I'm going over to the bar and you're going to let Mikhail know that a friend of Igor's is here to see him. If he still doesn't want to see me, you can throw me out. I won't fight it."

There was only a fraction-of-a-second pause before the man replied, "You must be checked."

I sighed and put the cigarette pack and lighter on the nearest table. I held out my arms and waited while he patted me down. The search was thorough except for the fact that he left the cigarettes and lighter alone. The silent doorman never looked at me, nor did he look away; he had a sense of dreamy awareness.

After my search, the bodyguards went to inform Mikhail about my presence. I picked up my things and walked to the bar. I slapped the mahogany surface hard with my palm. "Vodka, comrade. Nothing cheap, either. Mother Russia's finest," I demanded in a happy tone. I wanted these men to think I was a joke — pushing them with North American ignorance would help.

The bartender killed me twice with his eyes, but he fetched the drink with robotic efficiency. Moments later, I heard the quiet footsteps of the returning doormen and watched them, out of the corner of my eye, take seats at a table ten feet from me. Their distance and looks of disgust meant I was about to meet Mikhail.

After a minute, I was joined at the bar by a sandy-haired man in his early forties. He sat lower than me on the bar stool. I estimated he was about five-eight. He seemed fit, and there was a U-shaped scar under his right eye. He had been a fighter once. The signs never left.

"Who are you?" Mikhail's voice had no accent but it seemed to command respect.

"You sent two boys to kill me earlier. I want to talk about it."

If my words hit a nerve or shocked Mikhail, he didn't show it. He turned his head slightly and looked closely at me. I put the cigarette pack on the bar and lit the only remaining cigarette.

"Was it the *boys* who told you to come here?" Mikhail put some edge on the word *boys;* the edge told me they would be dead by morning.

"I want to know why I'm on your radar, and I want to know how to work this problem out," I said.

"It is very admirable of you to try and parlay peace, but it is in vain. You were stupid to come here. All you have saved is the cost of the gas it would have taken to find you again."

Mikhail had confirmed I was on his shit list, and that I needed to get higher up the on the food chain before I could bargain. "Call Sergei and ask him what he thinks. See if my being here, and the fact that I'm not dead yet, changes anything. If not, I'll pay up, and we can settle this now."

"I will not be calling anyone. You made a huge mistake and I will not be doing the same." His hard eyes watched me the whole time he spoke.

I pulled out my wallet. The movement caused no alarm with Mikhail; he knew I had been frisked before I sat down. The bodyguards moved closer, about five feet behind me. One was to my right, the other to the left of Mikhail. I pulled the fake credit card free and put my wallet away.

I took the first drag off my cigarette and said, "I'll pay up and we can get started."

Mikhail smiled, as if my gesture was amusing. I looked into his eyes and felt the left side of my face pull into a cold grin — my uncle's grin. I took another drag of my cigarette and put the glowing tip into the hole in my pack of cigarettes. The package immediately began to expand. I had it airborne, on its way to Mikhail's face, by the time it exploded. His scream shocked the bodyguards, but they didn't draw their guns right away. The two men were street toughs; they never prepared for being attacked. They only thought they had to look scary. The fireball had confused them. They didn't know whether to protect the boss or kill me. The exploding condom set Mikhail's hair and coat on fire; his lips let out a shriek as he rolled, burning, on the floor. The credit card hung low in my right hand as I covered the five feet between the bodyguards and myself. The guard on the right saw me coming; he shrugged back his coat and reached across his body. I used my left palm to mash his gun hand against his chest, suppressing his draw. The card was edge out in my hand as I punched across the bodyguards shoulder, being sure to tag the side of his neck. The spray of blood that followed meant I hit the carotid artery. The second guard was faster and already had his hand across his chest. I took the first guard, now a crimson fountain, by his lapels and pushed the both of us like a battering ram into his partner. The second man had freed his gun from the holster, but the bleeding guard rammed into him and trapped the gun between their bodies. I dropped the card and took advantage of the guard trying to plug the leak in his throat. I pulled his gun from the exposed holster and shot through his body four times.

I kicked the second guard's gun away from his body and checked both men for signs of life. I turned away from the dead bodies when I heard a sizzle from behind me. The bartender had squirted water from his bar sink onto Mikhail to put him out. I shot the bartender square in the chest, sending water shooting up to the ceiling. Mikhail was the only one left; his curses and moans mingled with the smells of gunpowder and burning hair. I walked over to him and pulled out the cell phone I took off of Igor.

"Dial Sergei and tell him I want out of this."

"Sergei doesn't make deals. This ch . . . changes nothing." His voice had lost its tone of authority after the fire on his head went out.

"Look around, Mikhail. Everything has changed. Sergei might not make deals, but I'll float one your way. Make the call, and I'll move on."

I dropped Igor's cell phone on the bar and righted a stool. I took a seat and waited while Mikhail got up off the floor. Parts of his face and scalp were blistered, and a good portion of his neck was seared. He picked up the phone and dialled. I watched him press the buttons and committed the number to memory.

The feeling of the pistol on the burned skin of his neck froze Mikhail solid. "Put the phone on speaker, and keep it English."

Mikhail sniffed hard and spat out a glob of black fluid onto the floor. "I have to ask for Sergei in Russian or I won't be put through."

"Make it quick. This is not the time to get ideas."

I listened to Mikhail spit out a machine-gun sentence in Russian. I pressed the gun hard into his burned scalp, forcing him to keep the Russian short. He ended his sentence and waited nervously for a reply.

"*Da?*" The phone belched out a thick Russian voice.

"Sergei, there has been a complication."

"*Da?*" The same word, but a new meaning — something entirely different than yes. The quiet word spoke loud vol-

104

MIKE KNOWLES

umes, demanding explanation, apology, and appeasement.

"The two men I sent failed, and now the thief has killed three men here at the club."

"*Da?*" This last word was chiselled out of concrete. It was a short word, but its slow delivery made it seem like a harsh rebuke.

"Yes, he wants to know what can be done to . . . make this right."

There was no cryptic reply right away. The pause could be good or bad. It could be a thought or it could be the silence of a multitasker. The silence someone would need to send more men to the club.

"He is there with you now?"

"Yes, Sergei. He is listening."

"Something was taken . . . information. I want it back," Sergei said.

"The information is out of my hands now; it's been passed on and probably dissected," I said.

"*Nyet*. This information was . . . unique. The men who wanted it would not show it to many people. I am told the information was encrypted, and those who stole it will not be able to see what it is right away. It will take time, the proper tools, and expertise to make sense of it. You say you want this to be over. Regain this information you stole, along with any equipment used to decode it, and all will be forgotten. This must be done by tomorrow."

"Tomorrow is too fast."

"*Da?* What you want is expensive. The only way you can pay is through immediate results."

I had an opening. It wasn't much, but it was something. "If I get everything you want, we're clean no matter what?"

After a long pause Sergei replied, "No one will come for you again, and we will not look for you. But if you do not succeed, more will come and they will not be children. I know of one person in particular who would like to speak with you."

I remembered the huge Russian I shot, and the office that had been wiped out. "Whatever. Twenty-four hours and *all* will be forgotten?"

"*Da.*"

My grin returned, but Mikhail didn't notice. The gunshot that came next filled the room. Mikhail's body was pitched from the stool.

"Mikhail?" Sergei's voice was louder but unconcerned.

"Dead," I said. "It doesn't matter, though. In twenty-four hours you will have forgotten him. *Da?*"

"*Da,*" was the only reply I was given. I was sure it sounded more like "dead."

powered down the small, now-silent phone and put it into my pocket. The phone would be my only untraceable way to contact Sergei again. I picked up a bar rag and wiped the gun I had used, and then I put it into Mikhail's hands. The scene wouldn't hold up as a murder-suicide when the police looked at the ballistics, but it would steer attention away from a homicide by an outsider for a while. I used the rag to wipe down everything else I had touched and then I went through everyone's pockets. I used the bar keys I found on Mikhail to lock up, as though it were closing time on a slow night. I wiped the keys with my sleeve and let them fall into a storm drain as I walked past my car. I did a small loop around the block to make sure no one was coming or already following me. When I was sure I was clean, I made my way back to the car and drove away.

The drive went nowhere in particular for a while. I had to weigh out my options. The Russian mob was a growing force; they had fought Paolo and his Italians for years, and they showed no signs of weakening. They were getting stronger, and the capital they had meant they could afford to bring in heavy hitters — much heavier than Igor and Gregor. They would find me again if I didn't come up with the disks, and it would be tough to walk out of an ambush a second time. The disks would be hard to find. If they were difficult to read, Paolo would need to outsource the job. It would take someone with the know-how, and with mob connections. There could not be many people who fit those criteria in the city. The only issue became who to ask. Questions are like wraiths — they take on a life of their own and they linger. Whoever I asked would understand what went on when they found out the person I asked about happened to get roughed up that very same night. If I had to ask someone for information, I would have to be sure it couldn't lead back to me. It occurred to me during the drive that, almost at once, I had decided to steal back the information from Paolo. I would once again bite the hand that fed me. I thought about how I had fallen into this situation, and it made my head ache. The blood pulsed hard in my ears, and red ate away at the corners of my vision. I had been given a job that was more sensitive than I knew. No one had told me I was going up against the Russians; it was a suicide job. Then it hit me — this was Paolo's payback for what I had done. Paolo was finally going to take the Russians down, and he was going to use me to do it. It was fitting, considering it was my fault that violence had resumed after Tommy's death. I had judged the Russians wrong then. They were stronger than anyone knew and they welcomed open war in the streets. The Italians had fought for years since I helped kill Tommy Talarese; dozens of made men had been killed, and millions of dollars had been lost. When I reached out for information, Julian said he wanted to kill me but he wasn't allowed. That was because Paolo wanted the Russians to kill me. He had Julian send me where they were sure to pick me up. Paolo used the Russians against me just as I had used them against him. I'm sure he had some kind of goose-and-gander analogy he found amusing. I wondered if I had been strung along for years by Paolo, or if the situation presented itself and he unleashed the anger he had held in check since I helped free Sandra. I couldn't tell and I wasn't sure I would ever know. Deep down the only thing I was sure of was that it had been a mistake to work for a man like Paolo Donati.

Because I had been so well prepared for this life by my uncle, I had no connections outside my work. My uncle never brought anyone near the house. It might as well have been a space station; it was inaccessible to anything that operated in his working world. He met people in a coffee shop. The shop was owned by the daughter of a very well connected man, so nothing happened there except conversation. It was a franchise shop with a comical robin welcoming all inside the yellow and brown interior. The air was thick with smoke and the smells of coffee and baked sugar. The coffee shop was used as an office and my uncle checked in often. I came along every time, even if business was going to be discussed. Learning how to operate and who to operate with was all part of my education. Some days we were there alone for hours on end. If I was lucky, we sat at one of the tables that doubled as a video game. The thick plastic tabletop was scorched with cigarette burns and covered in a thick layer of grease from food and skin oil from filthy hands. It was the kind of table that destroyed the myth about a three-second rule for dropped food. Anything that touched that table was instant garbage.

I remembered my slippery fingers as I gripped the joystick under the tabletop. I moved Pac-Man around the table under the coffee mugs and plates away from ghosts constantly following me. My uncle encouraged the game as though it were a poor man's chess.

"Rules allow you to win at this game," he said. "Rules. Knowing your rules and theirs — knowing them makes the difference. Once you know their rules you can plan around them. Make their rules work against them. You understand, Will?"

I nodded my response, not daring to take my eyes off the screen. "Yeah," he went on. "The ghosts, they outnumber you, they always will, and if you kill one of 'em word gets back fast, and they send more. They're fast too, faster than you, but they have to follow the same paths as you do. That's how you get them, boy. They follow your trail. You have to make them think they know where you're going. Once you can make them think the way you want them to then you're in control. It doesn't matter if they have more people, or if they're faster. If you're in control they'll be where you want them to be. How can they ever touch you if you don't let them? The plan separates you and them. It makes any situation work in your favour. You plan right, you'll live through anything."

I didn't bother to look up from the screen; he didn't want me to anyway. I thought of my mom and dad. They died — the ghosts ate them whole. I thought about them as I pivoted in a corner, moving back and forth, waiting to be surrounded. Seconds before the armless ghosts touched me I ate the large white ball in the faded corner of the screen and turned the tables. I didn't fight the grin as I screamed over the ghosts, watching their eyes run home. The ghosts were reborn again and again while I ran.

"You use confrontation too much, boy. You always want to fight. Why fight at all when you could be somewhere else? All that fighting slows you down. It makes you slow, predictable. Those ghosts have the numbers to lose to slow you down. They always come back, and soon you'll be in a corner without an advantage."

I didn't answer as I set up in another corner to wait for the ghosts. I pivoted back and forth waiting on them. I watched the yellow and orange spectres close in, moving as one, almost on top of one another. I watched the pair approach and waited for them to enter the corner until one ghost broke from the path and moved to the other side of the corner. Watching the unexpected advance, I moved one step too far. The yellow ghost collided with me, and I watched the mouth of my Pac-Man roll back clockwise into oblivion. I stared at the greasy screen for a second before finally looking at my uncle. He wore a grin on his face. It was cold and scary.

"You got predictable, and the machine made you pay. I knew people who got predictable and it cost them a lot more than a quarter. You know people like that too."

My hands gripped the sides of the game table hard. They slowly slipped away from the edges, sliding on human grease.

"Don't get mad. It's a weakness someone will exploit. You need to be able to think without connection to your emotions. You need to be unpredictable."

I didn't answer.

"Do you want more quarters?"

I nodded, and he slid one across the table. It left a trail in the grime. "I'll keep giving you money to play, but you have to play my way. I want you to avoid all the ghosts. Don't kill any of them. If you do, the money stops."

I played for hours that day until my eyes were bloodshot and my mouth tasted like the foul air surrounding me. I died over and over again at first, but the quarters kept coming — leaving trails in the grease as though they were snails. I watched the table and learned slowly to think ahead of one ghost, then two, then three. After too many hours I began to see the whole table at once. I followed each ghost with my eyes, learning how they moved. Soon I learned how they reacted, and then I survived them. They couldn't touch me anymore. I made a choice not to let them. They floated nearby, but they never touched me.

My uncle ate in silence as I navigated the tabletop universe. I finally looked up after logging my initials into the high-score position for a fourth time. My name was written in a vertical strip under the plastic tabletop. My uncle's face had no grin this time. There was only a smile. "You played them all. They went everywhere you wanted them to go. You controlled them. You were the one in charge even though it's their game and they had the numbers. You can manipulate any situation in your favour. You just have to play it without emotions — without connection." He etched my initials into the table grease with his thumb. Then he got up to leave without saying another word.

I learned to embrace living without connection or emotion. I lived my life disconnected, surviving the world by calculating every move. Then, in one day, I destroyed all of my work, following Steve across town on his homicidal visit to the Talarese residence. I did it because I saw two people connected. Two people who didn't fight to stay below everyone's radar. I remembered two other people who did the same. I refused to let the ghosts take two people who, despite my best efforts, I had connected to. Steve was the closest thing I had to a friend, the closest thing to human contact I had, and I couldn't let that go.

I had tried to manipulate the situation, to see every angle and fight the odds, but I hadn't escaped unscathed. Our violence took too much, and left little to barter with. We had our lives, but I lost my work and my contacts. I spent my life avoiding relationships and connections, and now that life was a prison. I was a ghost on my own, my education slowly killing me.

I never had a graduation. I always spoke of learning from my uncle as though it was an education, but there was no final commencement. There was no ceremony with cap and gown, just gunshots inside a strip club.

I had spent years learning from my uncle, training to be like him. I learned from him, and people he knew who were like him. He introduced me to hard men and women who didn't mind passing on what they knew to a young kid, and through them I developed. I learned from a small man named Rev all I needed to know about guns. He wasn't a man of the cloth; he got his name from the old revolver he kept no more than a heartbeat away in an ankle holster. The little man showed me how to clean, modify, and fire every type of weapon on the street. I spent years in a gym learning from an ex-prizefighter turned enforcer how to really fight — dirty without remorse. Ruby Chu taught me how to grift and steal for months until I picked it up. I had done work-study with anyone who would take me, and it hardened the boy I was into something else. Something unlike everything I came from.

I worked the jobs my uncle scored. No one knew me outside of the people I learned from, and they weren't connected to the kind of work my uncle and I did. I never knew who supplied the work. I just knew that we worked every few months and that the jobs were always different: armoured cars, stores, even banks. Every few months I was told about a job and the planning started. I was never clued into the who or why, just the what and how.

Robbing the strip club was just another new experience to me. I never knew why the Hollywood Strip presented itself as a target worthy of our notice, or why it had to be only the two of us. I was just told it had to be done, so I started getting things ready without question.

We hit the club on a Wednesday. The second night of the week the club was open. I wanted to wait to do it closer to the big money nights, but I was overruled.

The Hollywood Strip had a regular schedule. The club closed at two but the customers never rolled out until half an hour after that. Two weeks of surveillance told me the girls went next. They left through a series of doors coming from an addition built onto the side of the building. The girls came out scrubbed clean in track suits. They looked like they could be regular mothers and wives — if they weren't out at almost three in the morning on a weekday. After the girls came the bartenders and bouncers; they left out the front door. The boss came out last with a final bouncer. The bouncer worked the floor inside and was first on the scene to deal with problems. He was big, well over six-five. His arms and chest were covered in soft flesh, which concealed a powerful frame. He looked like he was unnaturally strong his whole life, the kind of person who was a starter on the senior football team when he was only in the ninth grade. His back was wide — the width of two normal people — and his shoulders were piled high on his back muscles, making him look like he was constantly shrugging. The bouncer was big, but he was out of shape. His gut hung over his belt as though he were concealing a beach ball under his shirt. His head was bald, making the skin tags and lumpy growths on his face and scalp stand out. He was beyond ugly, and most people probably shied away out of equal parts fear and revulsion.

The bouncer walked the boss out every night. Together they punched in the security code and locked up. The owner, a tall Italian man with brown hair combed high on his head, would pull the doors twice after he turned the key, taking the repeated sound of metal on metal as proof the doors were locked. I had seen the owner up close several times when I was working surveillance. His sharp nose and flared nostrils sat below a pair or crazed eyes. His conversations were animated with anger and volume. He spoke constantly about himself, the trips he took, his athletic past, and repeatedly about his growing up in the neighbourhood without a father. He didn't wear suits; instead he wore different warm-up coats adorned with international soccer logos and his name, Rocco, embroidered on the back.

After three weeks of watching, we made our move once the last bartenders and staff drove away. The exterior of the building was painted black, making our dark clothes blend in. We leaned into a spot, between two pillars, used by a hot-dog vender every night until twelve. The cart was gone by the time we got there, but the space concealed us both from the door. The bushes in front of the walkway, which shielded the identity of clientele coming and going, protected us from the road. I held a heavy sap in my right hand, and I had to restrain myself from tapping it against my thigh while I waited. My uncle held a gun pointed at the pavement. His, like mine, was a reliable piece with no history. Guns were part of the job, but we rarely used them. My uncle thought guns brought too much heat, and they let the ghosts know where you were.

We waited twenty minutes for the owner and his body-guard to lock up. The mechanism on top of the door made a "ffff" sound, letting us know it was slowly pushing open. I heard the boss say in an angry tone, "I used to say what are those old fuckers complaining about? All they do is complain. But I tell you until you feel it you will never know. I can't do anything anymore — I'm too tired. I don't work out as much, and fucking — you can forget that."

A jingle of keys told me it was time to move.

"I went to the chiropractor yesterday and he's starting to work things out. The pain is out of my ass, but now it's down my leg to my toes. I tell you it kills to move them, but you got to. You got to move them to get rid of the pain. Tonight I won't get to bed until six, maybe later. That's how long it takes me to relax so I can sleep. But when I was young like you I thought these old guys . . ."

Rocco stopped talking when he saw me club the bouncer behind the ear. The ugly man's hands dropped the gym bag he carried, but he didn't fall. His knees wobbled and he shielded his head. I hit him again with the sap above the fingers he pressed against the first wound. He staggered again but he stayed up — out on his feet.

"Into the club." My uncle's voice was calm; it made it seem like agreement was natural.

We moved into the club without another word. My uncle was in first, covering the two men as they walked back through the door. When the door floated shut, I sapped the bouncer a third and fourth time behind each ear. His staggering stopped, and he went down on two knees before landing face first on the soiled carpet. I turned around and checked the street for anything strange before locking the door. It was then that Rocco got into it.

"You two are dead." His body shook with rage. "You disrespect me like this? Me? You think you two little fucks can rob me and get away with it? Do you know who I am? Do you know how long I've been here? Do you even know who owns this place? You're gonna disrespect me like this? I'm gonna bury you."

"Let's go to the office," my uncle said, his voice still even and calm.

"Fuck you. I'm not going anywhere. You think —" I cut him off, swinging the sap across his jaw. The blow was hard enough to turn his head and break some teeth, but not hard enough to knock him out. I shoved him through the club as he grabbed at his face.

"This way," I said, pushing the club owner, who was dribbling blood on the floor, in front of me. The locked door to his office read "Private." We ignored the sign and the lock, opening the door with the keys the owner kept in his front pocket. Inside I saw several more locks and chains that would keep the door locked from the inside. I remembered wondering why this guy would need to be locked up so tight in this room. I guessed it was for entertainment. I found out later I was wrong.

The room was done in dark grey. The carpet, walls, and couch were all shades of grey. The only interruptions to the grey came from the dark mahogany desk and the art on the walls, which was vibrant and colourful. Each picture depicted great athletic achievements in soccer and football.

"Open the safe." My uncle's voice was still calm and even.

To my surprise Rocco bent and began to open the large safe on the floor behind the desk. He held his jaw in one hand as he clicked the dial left, then right, then left again. He mumbled something that might have been a death threat through his damaged face, then swung the door open. The safe was full of money — a lot more than two nights' take. I loosened the canvas bag on my back and got to work without being told. I worked fast moving the bricks of bills from the safe to my bag.

"Now open the other one."

I paused for a second. *Other one? What other one?* I looked over my shoulder at my uncle. He stared at Rocco, who returned his gaze with his mouth open a little wider than the injury made necessary. My uncle cocked the gun and asked again. The club owner said nothing. My uncle walked closer to him and put the gun to his knee. "Open the other one now or I take the knee. After that it's the other one, then your balls."

I had never known my uncle to do anything like this. Usually he hired a crew so that we never needed anyone to open safes for us. Tonight we had done everything strange. We came on a weird night, and we had no safe man when it was apparent that my uncle knew there would be two safes. Rocco shook his head, and the gun went off. I stared at the two of them until my uncle yelled, "Get the money, boy!"

I got back to work, moving less methodically than I would have liked. The club owner rolled on the ground, mumbling in Italian at us both. My uncle held the gun to the other knee as blood and cartilage spilled onto the floor.

"Obay. Obay. I'll do it," he said through his battered mouth. Rocco dragged his body across the floor. My uncle kept his gun against Rocco's knee the whole way. Rocco opened a mini-fridge in the corner and ripped out the shelving. Leftovers from the buffet splashed out from inside the fridge. The club owner had shrimp on his shirt as he worked his hand deeper inside the fridge. I heard a squeak, and his hand came out with a black bound book. My uncle took the gun off his knee and took the book. Rocco sagged onto the floor. His head stayed in the fridge. My uncle balanced the book on the gun in his hand; his left hand flipped through the pages.

"Motber fubber," was all I heard before my uncle's chest exploded red onto the ceiling. I threw the canvas bag at the fridge and drew the gun from behind my back. I pulled the trigger four times, putting bullets into the side of the fridge and the man's chest. I dropped the gun and ran to check my uncle. He had no pulse, and his chest was

MIKE KNOWLES

not moving. For half a minute I panicked, looking frantically around the room for help that was not there. Something caught my eye and challenged the panic. I looked into my uncle's face and saw that it was blank — completely without expression. I stared at him and realized that he had done something different; he didn't plan this out, and it got him. The ghosts caught up with him in this dingy strip club. I refused to let the ghosts get me too. They had killed enough of my family. I put the book that lay beside his dead body into the duffle full of cash and put it over my shoulder. I picked up my gun and used a tissue from the desk to wipe it down as I walked out to the entrance. I found the body of the bouncer where I left it — face down on the floor. I pressed the gun into his palm, waited five seconds, and then I walked back to the office. I put the gun down under the desk and stowed my uncle's pistol behind my back. I picked up my uncle's body and walked out of the club past the body of the bouncer still on the floor.

An hour later in a remote part of the city, I burned the car we took to the job with my uncle in it. Once the car had charred, I used the switch car to push it into a murky pond. It wasn't a proper burial, but it was much more than other members of the family had gotten. I drove home with the money, the book, and no idea what I was going to do.

I rose the next day and without thinking went to my uncle's coffee-shop office. The newspapers detailed the manhunt for the ugly bouncer who was wanted for questioning about a murder at the Hollywood Strip as well on several outstanding warrants. There was no mention of other blood at the scene or a ballistics discrepancy. They must have been saving that as a way to identify the real killer.

On my third day in the shop, an older man joined me at my Pac-Man table, sitting down with a coffee and a doughnut. I stared up at him from the newspaper and watched as he dunked his doughnut into the coffee. I glanced around the room and noticed that there were a bunch of empty tables, but this old guy had chosen mine.

"Help you, old man?" I asked.

Between bites of doughnut the man spoke. "I gotta tell you, kid, you are a hard one to find. That uncle of yours told me nothing of how the job was going to go down, and when he botched it like he did I thought he ran out on me. But I got wind of a partner he used, and a place they held meetings in. Lucky for me I know the owner so I just had to wait for you to pop up."

"Who are you?" I asked.

"I'm the guy you owe something to," the old man said in a cold voice. He went on without waiting for me to respond. "It's like ants. You know ants, kid? No? Well, ants bring everything back to the hill — it's their job. You found some tasty sugar and you're sitting on it. What're you trying to do, make your own hill?"

"I don't know you, ant man," I said, confused.

"I set up the job you pulled. I gave you all of the details. Now it's time for you to give me my cut."

"This is some grift. You figure me here alone means my partner is dead, so you try to move in. I don't know you, old man, and I'm not buying any of this. Who are you, anyway?"

He took another bite of the doughnut and looked hard at me. "I don't explain myself to anyone, ever, but you're young, kid, so I'll give you a heads-up. My name is Paolo Donati. The place you robbed was mine. I set it up."

The name shocked me. On the street Paolo Donati was all kinds of trouble. He was primed to become boss over the whole city. A red flag went up in my head. Something was off.

MIKE KNOWLES

"If you are who you say you are, then why use us? You got plenty of people who work for you, why not use them?"

He put the last bite of doughnut into his mouth and looked out the window. He licked his fingertips and then spoke as he probed his molars with his index finger. "Like I said, it's like ants, kid. Most anthills have more than one queen. You know that? More than one? Well, if the ants see one queen is not able to function they will feed the other. Eventually it will die while the other takes over."

I didn't follow right away. It didn't matter because he continued, "That guy in the club was working for me, and it turned out he was trying to build his own anthill . . . without me."

I got it almost immediately. "He was screwing you out of money and doctoring the books. You used us so no one in your anthill would find out someone was taking advantage. Using us kept you secure in your position." I felt like an ass speaking about anthills, but the man across from me wasn't kidding.

"Yeah, kid, you got it. Now that we know who's who and what's what, let's get this straight. You owe me money and a book. I'm gonna tell you how much, and you're going to give me what I want. I'm going to pay you double for what you did because you killed that thief and framed that ugly bouncer. That worked out better for me than what your uncle planned."

"How much?"

He told me, and I looked out the window, screaming inside my head.

"Don't worry, kid, there's more money. I got lots of money, that is, if you want to work for it." That was the first time I went to work for Paolo. It would not be the last.

After Paolo had cut me loose for killing Tommy, I was left without a job again. I had spent so long living the way I had that there was little chance I could start over fresh. I only knew one kind of life, and that life gave me few options. I couldn't stay in the city — there would be no employment when word got out I was blacklisted, and solo jobs didn't have longevity. Working alone kept the jobs small and the risks high. No one retired from a career of working alone; coffins and cells are lined with cons who thought they could beat the system every time — by themselves. I needed to work my way into another network where I could find bigger jobs with other professionals. I knew of some names in Montreal, so I decided to scout out opportunities there.

I took a week and drove out to Montreal. I spent time in the right places asking for the wrong kind of people. After a few days of looking, the names I asked about sent a car for me. Some of the names I dropped from back home checked out, and I was told there could be work if I proved myself. Proving myself could have meant anything from murder to shooting up in front of an audience. There were all kinds of chest-beating rituals intended to sniff out undercover cops. I didn't trust anyone to set up a job for me, so I said I would think about it and let them know; they gave me a number to call when I had made a decision. I took a cab from the meeting and got out on Boulevard Saint-Laurent. The street, known as locally as "The Main," was full of bars, nightclubs, and restaurants. Even in the early evening the street was crowded with people trying to get a glimpse of the real nightlife of the city. The bloodbath in Hamilton forced me to operate with greater care because I had no idea when I could become a target for what I had done. A new city hundreds of kilometres away was no exception. I used the windows of every restaurant to check the posted menus, and to look behind me using the polished glass as a rear-view mirror. It didn't take me long to see that I was being followed by two men. The reflections I saw several times in the windows made me sure they were tailing me. Seeing two men at once usually meant trouble. One person is a good enough tail — if they're good. Sometimes two people worked together, leapfrogging after a target to lower the odds of the target recognizing a face. Two men together meant something else entirely; it meant there was going to be heavy lifting involved. If the two were pros there was probably a driver out there too, so the team could get away fast.

I stopped at a phone on the street and called the number I had been given at the meeting.

"*Oui?*"

"We just met. Do I have reason to think that there are *two* things you want to see me again about?"

The voice on the phone did not betray any emotion; it just shifted to accented English. "We are waiting for a call. That is it."

I clicked the phone down and kept walking, immersing myself deeper in the crowds. The men I met with denied knowing the two men behind me. It wasn't proof that the men belonged to some other outfit, but it was enough for me to know that they were there to start trouble. I moved quickly and entered the first mall I saw. I crossed the sensors of the first clothing store that appeared and picked a shirt, hat, and glasses from the nearest racks, tore off the tags, gave them to the cashier, and hit the change room. When I came out, I paid for my new outfit and browsed near the front of the store, using the window to look out into the mall. Through the spaces between the frosted letters in the glass I saw throngs of shoppers walking by. I could also see a man loitering by the mall entrance, cell phone in hand, meaning the other man was searching the mall for me.

I walked out of the store and went to the warm pretzel restaurant three stores to the right. I bought a pretzel and a Coke and sat at one of the tables provided out front. I was out of sight from the mall door, so I ate a few pretzels and waited twenty-five minutes. After the pretzels and Coke I got up and checked the door. No one was standing guard, cell phone in hand. I went deeper into the mall, found an ice cream shop, and ate for another half hour. When I finished the ice cream, I asked a girl at the information kiosk where the closest cabs were located. The girl behind the counter told me of an exit on the other side of the mall. On my way to the exit I spotted a mall rat. She was a teenage Goth kid hanging out by herself. She looked dirty — like one of the many homeless of the city. Montreal had a huge number of homeless teenagers who escaped their parents for the club life of the big city. I grabbed the girl by her arm, forcing her to join my pace.

"Hundred bucks if you leave with me."

"No way, loser. Get the fuck off me."

The crazy population of the city made sure nothing surprised this girl anymore. She didn't even seem scared of a strange man offering her money.

"No sex. No date. Just help me get out of here, and you can take the hundred bucks plus cab fare wherever you want to go."

"Why the hell would I go anywhere with you, asshole?"

"Either come or don't, but I don't have time to waste. One fifty, take it or leave it."

Her eyes lit up, and she licked her lips. "Fine. Where's the money?"

"You get it in the cab."

I didn't let her continue the conversation. We walked to

the exit and got into a waiting cab. The watchers were looking for one man in different clothes. All they would see leaving was an unhappy man dragging his daughter out of the mall.

"Airport," was all I said to the cab driver.

"*Oui.*"

Two blocks into the ride, I told the driver to pull over. I got out and left two hundreds on the seat. I walked away without saying another word.

I wasn't sure who would be looking for me, especially in Montreal. If I had to guess, it would be the cops. Criminal organizations were big business in Montreal; the city had Italians, bikers, even Russians of their own. The organized crime guys must have seen me leave a hot spot and tailed me for an ID. I moved around the city for a few more hours, checking for a tail, but I never found one. After I decided I was clean, I took a cab back to my car. I had stashed it at an expensive city parking-garage a block away from the motel I was staying in. I travelled light so all that was in the motel room was a change of clothes in a duffle bag. I decided to leave clean, dropping the motel key down a sewer grate before paying up for the car and driving home.

When I got back into town I checked my office and found only one change: there was a plain unaddressed white envelope on the floor inside the door. The letter contained a piece of paper with a phone number on it. The digits indicated it was a cell number. Out of curiosity, I dialled it.

"I was looking for you."

The voice registered immediately — it was Paolo Donati. Our conversation was short — all that was said was a meeting place and a time. I had to haul ass to make it out of the city to a small-town restaurant that served all-day breakfast. I got there first and took a corner booth where I could eye the exit. The booth would also give me a chance to slip into the nearby kitchen if need be. Kitchens are always busy, and fire codes mean they always have exits. I checked before I came in — the kitchen exit was on the right. It was a standard door, which would open easily so the kitchen staff could get to the Dumpster with their hands full. I carried the Glock inside a folded newspaper into the restaurant. I could have cared less about the news; the paper let me blend in, and it hid my gun in plain sight. I looked like any other customer, but I was one who could pull a gun without making any grand gestures.

As I sat, I scanned the restaurant. There was no one looking my way, no one on a cell phone, and no one who suddenly got up to use the rest room. It was an odd choice for a meeting place, but it seemed clean.

Right on time, Paolo Donati made his way into the restaurant. He was an old man, but he looked fit. His hard, pointed nose showed signs of being broken several times. His dark eyes were hard, and they scanned the room, taking everyone in while simultaneously sending out a don't-fuck-with-me message. He wore green slacks and a blue nylon golf pullover. He looked like a golfer from a distance. Up close, he looked like someone who had just robbed and stripped a man on his way to the links. He wore a heavy grey wool cap, like the old-time golfers wore; it covered the immaculate haircut that framed his head in silver.

His eyes spotted me right away but went over the room twice more. A passing waitress saw him looking and said, "Just grab a seat, hon, I'll be right with you."

He didn't miss a beat; he gave her a sweet smile and said, "I just saw my friend. I'll be fine. Thank you, dear."

He didn't stroll with the languid gait I had seen on

many occasions. He shuffled like a man his age should have walked.

"Nice walk," I said as he approached.

"It helps to blend in."

I shook my head. "You don't blend in. The golfer's outfit is wrong. You'd look better in a casual suit. Like a guy with money who still likes the simple stuff," I said.

All I got was a cold stare for a reply. We sat silent, waiting to order, then continued to say nothing while we waited for our food. Finally, after the food arrived and the waitress left, Paolo told me why we were there.

"I fired you for good reason."

"No argument here. It could have been much messier," I said.

"Everyone thinks you're out with me."

"I *am* out with you."

"You aren't out of shit, *figlio.*"

I knew the word *figlio* meant *son.* I heard enough Italian over the years to decipher bits and pieces. Whatever the translation, he used the word like a boot, shoving me down into my place.

"I let you off. Never forget that. You didn't earn, justify, prove, or bribe anything from me. I decided your fate. You breathe because I had a single thought that you might be useful."

I took in the rant and thought it over. What he said wasn't false. The only missing part would have been the expense of killing me. It would have been hard, costly, and pointless. "The point is I'm out," I said between sips of tea.

"Fuck, you really are stupid, aren't you. You are what I say you are, and no one is going to hire you until I decide I'm done with you. Not even those bilingual criminals. Oh, don't look surprised, I know all about the little introduction you had. It's good you came home because I was ready to make sure no one would be looking to give you work."

I took another sip of tea. The man across the table controlled my immediate future; he could make things easy or very, very hard. I decided to hear him out.

"What's on the table, Paolo?" I asked.

He smiled then. It was the smile a cat would have on its face when the mouse finally gave up and stopped running. I hated that look and I promised myself I would remember it, and someday pay it back.

"We on a first-name basis all of a sudden? You and me equals now? What part of the city is yours? 'Cause I own fucking everything. Now shut up and listen. You're gonna work for me like before, but this time no one will know you fucking exist."

I had to admit I liked how this was going. It already sounded natural to me.

Paolo went on, "A man like me is always surrounded by people who are looking to take information and put it to use. Many people in my own organization would take me down if they could. I need someone no one would trust. Someone with no allegiances who will work jobs I set up. You'll get things for me, private things, on people who work for and against me, and you'll deal only through Julian. That way I stay on top, and you stay employed. And if you get an idea to rip me off, to take from me? Well, I got an army who would love to know what really happened to Tommy."

"I'm not going to become a contract killer for you."

"I want information only. I don't need you to kill anyone."

"How much does it pay?"

"More."

Paolo didn't wait for me to say yes. He stood up.

"Thanks for breakfast, *figlio*. Julian will be in touch."
And he walked out.

I paid for breakfast. *What the hell?* I figured. *I have a job. I can afford it.*

had a cramped timetable for getting back what I had already stolen. The Russian demand of twenty-four hours didn't give me enough time for finesse. I had no idea who Paolo Donati would contact to hack some encrypted disks. If I started asking around it would take longer than a day to find out, and word of it would leak up, leaving me blocked out or dead. My only option was to go at the problem head-on. I had to find someone in the know and grind what I needed out of them. I also had to get the information in a way that wouldn't leave any traces back to me. It would not be in my best interest to make things right with the Russians only to have more problems with the Italians. Paolo wanted me dead. I didn't know why he chose now to pay me back, but his intentions were clear. I had to weather the storm with the Russians so I could settle up with Paolo later.

I really only had one name to choose from — Julian. Julian was Paolo's second; he knew where all the bodies were buried. Julian would know who the disks were sent to and why. He wouldn't appreciate being squeezed, so I would have to make it hard on him. If I did it right, he would keep his mouth shut. If Paolo found out that Julian gave up information to me, he'd have the life expectancy of milk in the sun. Julian would have to keep quiet about what I did and wait for a time to deal with me privately.

After the business with Steve and Sandra, I had decided to find out where all of the major players lived. I knew where Julian lived, but there were few times when he was alone and unaccounted for. He worked whatever hours Paolo worked, and Paolo was a workaholic. The hours Julian spent at home in his condo were sporadic. Julian's condo also offered a high degree of security: there were guards in the building, in addition to whatever measures of his own he took to secure his home. I'd have to hit him between point A and point B. Point A was the restaurant; point B was his condo. I looked at my watch. It was 9:30 p.m. I still had time to do what needed to be done.

I took a cab from outside the office to the local hockey rink, which was always busy at night with games of shinny going on into the early morning. I stole an old Ford pickup with a large empty bed and headed away from the city to a garden centre on a back road in a quiet neighbouring town. It was still warm enough that a lot of the supplies were kept outdoors. I picked the padlock on the gate out front, drove in, and parked the truck beside a pile of garden stones. I piled as many of the huge garden stones as I could into the bed of the truck. Each stone pushed the shocks farther and farther down on the wheels. With the truck full, I drove out of the lot and onto the shoulder of the road. In the glow of the rear lights of the truck, I relocked the gate. I got back behind the wheel and headed back into the city. The truck lurched like a drunk, but when the odometer hit fifty the pickup was as solid as a sledgehammer.

I drove to the restaurant and parked in a lot on the corner; the dashboard clock read 11:23. I could see Julian's car parked out front. It was a Cadillac sedan, black, tinted, powerful, and fast. There was another vehicle parked out front: the black Escalade that transported Paolo everywhere he went. The fact that there were two cars in front of the restaurant told me Julian would be driving himself home eventually.

I spent the next two hours waiting in the silent truck staring at the two vehicles in front of the restaurant. At 1:13 there was finally movement. The lights went out in the windows, and the doors opened. Two men in suits came out first; they scanned the area before nodding towards the door. Three men left the restaurant and joined the two; among them were Paolo and Julian. Paolo got into the back of the suv with another man, and the two men in suits got in front. Julian waited alone in the street and watched the car pull away. He stood in the street for a full minute, waiting for something I couldn't see, then he walked to the Cadillac and shoved his body in. The car rocked from the impact of his huge body against the frame. I started the pickup and drove around the block.

The truck lurched forward, building speed slowly. After a minute, I was moving above the speed limit. I hung a left on a one-way street and used the road to connect to the street Julian would be taking. The truck slid a little as I rounded the corners, and there was a hard jolt when I pressed the gas pedal down to accelerate again. Pedal to the floor, I moved up the road looking for the black Cadillac. As if the heavens were looking down on me, I saw the car, alone, stopped at a light two hundred metres ahead.

As I approached the intersection I craned my neck to check the cross streets, saw no one coming. I yanked the wheel left and then hard to the right and swerved the weighted truck through the intersection like a right hook into the driver's side of Julian's car. I pulled my hands up to my face and shielded my head as the two cars collided. The impact shot through my body, and I felt ribs strain under the pressure of the seat belt. The frame of the old truck held, and I woke up after what felt like a long blink to find my legs still able to move, and the engine still clucking.

I pulled the emergency brake and kicked the dented side door open. I freed the gun from behind my back and held it with two hands as I approached the window of the Cadillac and looked inside. The window was shattered and the air bag had deployed, but no Julian. I bent to look deeper in the car and saw his body half out the passenger-side window. The direction of the impact and lack of seat belt had sent him flying sideways. The side impact beams kept Julian inside and the shape of the car somewhat recognizable, but the sheer force of the impact must have rocked Julian hard. Quickly I moved to the opposite side of the Cadillac. Julian's head and shoulders were out the passenger side window; he was semi-conscious and no good to me. He mumbled something in Italian through his bloody face when his glazed eyes saw me. I swore at him under my breath for not buckling up, then put him all the way out with the butt of the Glock. Killing Julian would let everyone know that the accident wasn't just a simple hit and run, and it wouldn't take long for Paolo to tie the hit on Julian to the disks; they would be gone forever after that. There were no cars nearby, but a set of lights approached in the distance. I reached in through the window and did a quick frisk. I pocketed Julian's wallet and a cell phone, and went back to the truck. I pulled myself in behind the wheel, leaving the broken door open. I released the emergency brake and put the truck in reverse. The engine chugged, but the truck made a choppy lurch back, slamming the broken side door into place. I moved away from the Cadillac and drove straight down the street. After a minute, I passed a car; the driver's stare at the wrecked front end of the truck was illuminated for me in the streetlights. I pulled a right as soon as I could and got off the main road. I found a parking lot a hundred metres from the road behind a closed Pizza Pizza, shut off the truck, and used my sleeve to wipe down the interior. I left the truck there and found a cab two blocks away. Police cars, sirens blaring and lights flashing, passed the cab on their way to the mess I left behind.

I changed cabs a few times to make sure no one was following me and got back to the office at 2:17 a.m. I put my gun, Julian's wallet, and the phones I took from Igor and Julian on the desk, then looked for whatever food I had on hand. I found some mixed nuts and a Coke. I ate and drank with relish before I even considered the phones. When I finished the food, I looked at Julian's phone. It was a slim model — modern and new. I pulled up the call history and clicked through until I found the date of the airport robbery. I checked the call log and saw that Julian had called a cell number minutes after I handed him the bag.

I took a deep breath and called the number. After six rings I got a sleepy, "Hello?"

"You done with the disks yet?" I asked in a gruff voice.

"What the fuck? Who is this?"

I asked again, and after another foul response I hung up. I went back to the call log and found the next number Julian had called that day. I tried the second number and got a much better response.

"Julian? I told you it'd take at least a week. Why are you calling me now?" There was a pause, then a hushed whine: "Aw, jeez, ya woke up Ma, now she's gonna be pissed."

I worked hard to make my voice deeper like Julian's

and I tried to talk like him. "Listen, I got another disk with some things the boss said would help. Codes he said you'd need. Important information. But it can't be dropped off. These shits we took it from are looking hard at us. I need to hand it off to you. You need to meet me this morning. Now."

The whiny whisper took on a scared tone. "Look, Julian," said the Voice, "I don't mean no disrespect, but I can't get involved with that. I promised Ma I was clean now. Aw, crap. Hold on." His words were muffled under a cupped hand as he told his mother that the call was a wrong number and he was just hanging up.

When the Voice came back I decided to press my luck. "Fine," I said. "I got an idea that will work out. Something no one will expect. No one will see this coming. I'll FedEx the disk to you. Give me your address."

There was a pause. "Julian? You know where I live."

There was a hint of question in the words, so I turned up the volume. "Who the fuck are you? You say no to me and I let it slide. I don't even press you. I decide to help you out 'cause I feel bad for your ma, and you start questioning me? You gotta make a choice, A or B, it's up to you. You can either worry about your mother or yourself, because in a few seconds I'm gonna find someone else to do your job, and then I won't care so much about you . . . or your mother."

"Julian . . . I . . . Julian, I'm sorry I —"

"Shut the fuck up. Stay quiet. Don't say anything to me. Just listen. I'm not the fucking post office. I can't send shit without all of the information that they want on the label. I want the address, the postal code, everything. Now!"

It all came out as soon as I finished yelling. Once the Voice stopped pleading and gave me what I asked for, I was moving. I picked up Julian's wallet and Igor's cell phone off my desk and opened the closet. I pulled a black windbreaker over my untucked shirt and pocketed a black watch cap. I removed the panel in the back of the closet and put in the wallet and cell phones. I took the sawed-off shotgun out for the second time, sliding it under my arm. Then I went back to my desk and used a Swiss Army knife to cut two holes into the material of the watch cap. I pulled it on and checked my vision through the holes. After a little adjusting and finger tearing, I had clear vision through the hat. I rolled the cap and put it in my back pocket. I stowed the Glock behind my back and flattened the back of the jacket over the holster.

My shoulders were starting to knot from the collision. I was tired and wanted nothing more than to eat then sleep for a month. But I couldn't stop, I couldn't slow down. If I lost momentum, I would lose the element of surprise — the only edge I had. I did two minutes' worth of stretching to loosen my shoulders and back. The final stretch was to get a bottle of Advil. I put four of the sweet tablets into my mouth and chewed them as I walked out of the office.

In the car, I drove just above the speed limit. I didn't want to draw any cop's attention. I was just another poor schlub off a late shift trying to get home a little quicker. The address the Voice gave me was on the other side of town. I pushed my way through the sparse traffic towards the Voice and his mother wishing I could slow down, but knowing I couldn't. The call put the Voice on edge, and I had to get there before the whimpering fear I yelled into him turned into afterthoughts that would question the whole phone call. I found the building and circled it twice, looking for heads illuminated in cars by my headlights. Those types of heads are like alligator eyes above the water, watching in dark silence for anything to come too close. I saw no one watching, and no one waiting, so I parked around the side of the building and got out. I opened the trunk and hid from the streetlight behind the open lid. From under a blanket, I retrieved the sawed-off shotgun and slid it up the side of my windbreaker so I could hold it tight to my body with the side of my bicep. I closed the trunk and walked around to the front of the high-rise. My walk was odd; the bulges from the watch cap and pistol clashed with the awkward gait caused by holding a shotgun to my body using my elbow.

I eyed each car I passed, looking for anything strange, but everything seemed clear. I took one last look around as I made a right off the sidewalk up to the Voice's building. Like most inner-city apartment buildings, this one had two sets of glass doors: one to enter the building from the street, another to the entryway that contained the elevators. The inner doors were sealed from the elements, and the old fan above pumped in the thick, untreated city air. I entered and simultaneous scents of cooked food, exhaust, and sweat filled the glassed-off partition like a gas chamber. There were no night watchmen or innocent bystanders in this building; the building was too poor and unsafe for either. I looked up and around and saw no cameras and no security system. The only sign of technology was the intercom, and that had a fist-sized hole in it. Through the smudges on the glass, I could see a stairwell and an elevator that would lead to the twelfth-floor apartment I was looking for. After one more look around, I made my awkward walk back to the car. I opened the trunk again and pulled a crowbar up from under the blanket. I shut the trunk and then wedged the crowbar under my left arm. I held it up pressed against my left side, forcing my walk to be even more constricted. Witnesses would remember the odd walk more than any other physical details. They would also not be concerned enough at the sight of me to call the police because they saw no evidence of a crime; they just saw another fellow resident afflicted by life in Hamilton's hard core.

The walk back was uneventful. Once inside the first set of glass doors, I let the shotgun slip down into my hand so I could place it on the dirt-caked floor mat. I let the crowbar loose next and forced it into the space between the inside doors. I pushed it in, wiggling it back and forth until I had it jammed far enough in to support some pressure. In one hard motion, I bent the metal door frame and cracked the glass, but with the destruction came a satisfying movement to the door. I picked up all I brought, concealed it once again, and hit the stairs.

On floor twelve, I opened the stairwell door quietly and checked the hall. No sound came through the crack in the door. The artificial ceiling light created the quality of perpetual midday. I waited a full three minutes in the stairwell, watching for any sign of life. When I was convinced there was none, I entered the hall and moved towards apartment 1207. I stopped in the hallway when I came upon the elevator. I pushed the button and waited, listening to the grinding of gears. Moments later, an artificial chime signalled the elevator's arrival. I stood off to the side and waited while the metal doors opened. No sounds came from the elevator car. I looked in and saw it was empty of people and cameras. I waited until the doors started to close; there was no sound letting anyone know it was about to happen, just an abrupt shifting of machinery and a scraping of metal on metal. I pushed the doors back open and used the crowbar to wedge them ajar. Satisfied that the bar would hold, and that no one would be using the elevator, I moved down the hall to 1207. At the door I listened carefully for any sounds from inside. I heard the faint sounds of a television, but I couldn't be sure if it came from inside or next door.

I stood a step away from the doorknob and moved my eyes over the locks. There were two locks: one standard mechanism above the doorknob, and a much heavier deadbolt a few inches above that. There was no way to account for a door chain on the other side. I didn't think there would be one — usually the chains are only on doors with three or more locks. One extra lock means cautious, but not paranoid. Most cautious people buy deadbolts and self-install them to save money. This lock was more than likely self-installed because no self-respecting lock-smith would put a deadbolt in crooked. It looked like a shit job, but the lock itself was a quality heavy-duty item. I couldn't waste time trying to pick the locks. The hallway was too bright for me to be inconspicuous, and the noise of the picks in the two locks might put the Voice on to me. I looked away from the locks to the door frame; it looked old. I dug into the wood with my thumbnail, and a piece came off with ease. The two steel locks were sitting in old rotted wood. Whoever put the second lock in never thought about how the door frame would handle the stress of being assaulted.

I stepped back from the door and took one last look down the hallway before rolling the watch cap over my head. I adjusted it with my one free hand until I could see clearly through the holes I made. I lowered the shotgun from under my jacket and rolled my shoulders to get the kinks out from the awkward posture I had been holding. Once I felt loose and my breathing was controlled, I stepped back until my back touched the opposite wall. The hallway gave me only four or five good steps from one side to the other. I moved back and forth over the distance twice, working on getting a rhythm to my steps and my foot placement. On my second practice, I let my foot extend within inches of the door, aiming six inches to the left of the two locks. Then, crossing the floor for the third time, I hit it.

The impact of my foot drove the door inward. The bolts tore, like blunt claws, through the old wood frame. I planted my foot inside and used my shoulder to take the impact of the door swinging back on itself.

The room was dark, and the light from the hallway spilled in, illuminating the small tiled entryway I was standing in. In front of me was a closet. To the right the tile continued into a bathroom, lit only by a faint night light. A flicker from my left brought my eyes and the shotgun over to the television, which was casting soft light onto a couch where an old woman sat. The flickering glow of the television made the wrinkles on her frightened old face stand out.

"You must be mom," I said. "Sit there and don't move."

I used my free hand to push the front door closed. The exposed bolts caught on the splinters they left when they tore free, and the door stayed closed. The woman on the couch stared at me, unflinching. Ahead of me I saw an alcove kitchen and two doors. One of the doors slammed shut. I sprinted across the room and kicked the door open. Inside, staring at me, a young Italian man was frantically dialling a phone. I gripped the shotgun with both hands and drove the stock into his face. The blow knocked him off of his feet straight onto his back like he had fainted.

I scanned the room fast. A heavy desk lamp was the only light source. Two laptop computers were on an old brown desk set that looked cheaply painted, and an old stained futon rested against the left wall. There was no other furniture in the room. The only decorations were posters — Pacino as Scarface and a porn star staring out from the wall with seductive eyes. I looked on the desk for the disks but saw only DVD cases, paper, and a few photos in frames. I recognized a face in one of the frames and hesitated for a second. The face was with four others, all of them gazing out from a soccer field. The five young men looked sweaty, tired, and happy. One kid held up his finger, wordlessly telling everyone they were number one. I knew the kid and his face. I thought about the features, the dyed blond hair, the patchy stubble, and the small mouth. I had seen the features at the airport; they belonged to Nicky — the amateur bagman I stole the disks from. Before he and his co-workers had been cleaned by the Russians, Mike had told me no one knew why Nicky volunteered to do the trade at the airport. He said no one had done anything like that before so no one challenged him; they were probably relieved that anyone volunteered. It was clear now that the amateur had set up his own scam with Paolo and his crew through his friend the Voice. The bagman had been out for himself, and he had set up a deal with Paolo that cut his friends and the Russians out of the loop. The Voice was the link back to the beginning.

I spoke at the rapidly blinking eyes staring up at me from the floor. "Give me the disks now." The voice I used had a terrible Russian accent attached to it.

"I don't know . . ."

I kicked him hard in the groin, and he curled up tight, screaming. I used the shortened barrel of the gun to straighten him out. "The disks, or I take your foot, then your mother's." The accent was better the second time.

"In . . . in . . . in the desk," he told me.

I opened the drawer and saw several unmarked CDs. I had to be sure they were what I needed. I cocked the shotgun and turned to the quivering mass on the floor. I took aim at his foot and took a slow, loud breath.

"Okay, okay they're in the floor."

"Get," was all I said, hoping my surprise didn't leak through.

The kid slid onto his belly and crawled toward the futon. He yanked free a patch of flooring and pulled a worn and battered lockbox from a space below the floor. I smiled under the mask just before I spun wildly.

# CHAPTER ELEVEN

M y body whirled in a circle and I fell toward the futon. The bullet in my left arm made me a human dreidel. I shot back through the door with both barrels and saw the body of the old woman leave her feet. The revolver she held fell sideways out of her hands onto the floor. In my haste I had written her off, and as a reward she shot me.

"Ma!" The Voice screamed as he lunged off the floor. I couldn't stand fast enough so I grabbed his legs as he ran to the door. I pulled him to the floor and began clawing up his legs toward his torso. He was wild, and I was shot. Holding him was impossible, so I used my head. I rammed my head into the back of his skull, hard, taking away some of his spunk. The second and third head butts made his body slacken.

I got to my feet and grabbed a pillow from the futon. I used the pillowcase to carry the shotgun, lockbox, and the two laptops. I walked out the door without looking at Ma and found the crowbar still in place in the elevator; I got on and kicked it free. As I descended, I put the crowbar into the pillowcase. When I straightened up, I caught sight of myself in the reflective surface of the doors; the left arm of the windbreaker was taking on a wet sheen. My arm was starting to hurt, and I was starting to feel faint.

I managed to get to the car without passing out. I clumsily held the bag and the back of my left arm with my right hand the whole way. The blood soaked between my fingers and rolled down the nylon fabric of the jacket. I pulled off the watch cap and folded it over, then worked it up under the coat until it was over the wound. The placement made me wince, but I pushed hard on the wound, hoping to slow the blood flow.

The keys were slippery in my fingers, but I got the car started. After three blinks, which took twelve semi-conscious seconds, I put the car in drive and watched the apartment building roll by the passenger window.

The driving was hard. I used my injured arm to hold the bottom of the steering wheel while my good arm held the dampening hat to the bullet hole. Every now and again I had to use both arms to painfully turn a corner. I drove, too slow, all the way to Sully's Tavern.

I pulled to the curb right in front of the door. It took me three tries to pull the keys from the ignition. On the third try I used my nails to get enough friction to pull the bloody keys from the steering column. I opened the door and took far too long to realize that the rhythmic beeping I heard was coming from the car I had just turned off — the lights were still on. I fumbled with the lights and got them off after two attempts with slick fingers. When I got to the tavern door the lights were off. Ten feet to the right was the door to upstairs. I walked to the door; it took sixteen small steps. I leaned on the buzzer for half a minute.

MIKE KNOWLES

When I released the button, it was red with blood. A voice greeted me, sleepy and pissed off.

"Huh?"

"Steve, it's Wilson . . . I need . . . help here."

The door buzzed, and I pulled it open. Steve was already coming down the stairs in a pair of boxers. His hard body, menacing in the stairway light, contrasted with his shaggy bed hair; he looked like a clown in a prison yard.

He helped me up the stairs to the kitchen. "You need to move my car and wipe it down, your door buzzer too. There's a bag and a gun on the seat. I need them . . . please."

Steve left wordlessly while Sandra, in a robe, pulled the windbreaker off me. It crinkled and cracked with caked dry blood. Sandra had seen cuts and bruises, but never bullet holes. She took a long look at me then stood and went to the phone.

"No doctors."

"But you're shot. I can't help you. You need a doctor. You could die."

"I know people who can take care of it, but not tonight," I said.

She took a deep breath and let it out slowly. "What can I do?" Her voice sounded defeated but also a little angry.

"Just tape gauze around it and cover it in plastic wrap. Try to clean me up so I don't look shot."

"You look like hell," she said. "You're pale, white as a ghost."

"Sandra, please, just help me. I'll be okay. I have a job to finish, then I'll get some help."

Pissed, Sandra left the room and came back with two washcloths, gauze, medical tape, and alcohol. She cut the shirt off me with kitchen scissors and used the washcloths to clean the blood off my upper body. Steve came in and put the pillowcase down by the door as Sandra was trying to tape gauze to the wound. The gauze had fallen off twice, and she kept having to start again. Wordlessly Steve understood. He pushed the gauze down hard and helped Sandra tape. I grunted with the pain of Steve's first aid, but he never let up.

When they had taped the gauze down I said, "Plastic wrap."

Steve went to the counter as Sandra spoke. "Why do you need that?"

"If you put it on tight and tape it down it will hold everything together and make it less bulky under a shirt. It will hide what happened," I said.

"Why would you want to hide it?"

"So no one else finds out it happened and tries to do the same thing again," Steve said.

His answer summed up the issue and it was good enough for Sandra. She used one hand to tilt my neck so she and Steve could wrap over my shoulder. This time Sandra wasn't as afraid, or tender. Nothing fell on the floor; she pushed hard with the plastic wrap, making sure the dressings would hold.

"Car hid?" I asked.

"Yep," was all he said as the box of plastic wrap went around and around my bicep.

The bullet had hit me high in the back of the arm. I couldn't see a hole in the front, so the slug still had to be in the meat of my arm. The nature of the wound meant that I could still lift my arm and move it in toward my body using my bicep, but any pushing movement was out of the question.

Steve spoke so quietly it was hard to hear him over the hum of the fridge. "The arm looks like shit. You can't leave it like this."

MIKE KNOWLES

"It won't be like this long," I said. "Can I get a shirt off you?"

Sandra left the room without a word. Seconds later, I heard drawers opening and slamming. She came back with a high school sweatshirt.

"No good. People will know it's not mine, and it could be traced back to you. I need something like a plain long-sleeve shirt, dark just in case blood leaks through."

She left the room again without a word. "She's pissed," I said. Steve didn't respond. "Where's the car?"

"Around back. Beside the Dumpster. You can't see it from the road."

"It won't be there long. In the morning I need some pants, new ones, yours are too small. After that I'm gone."

Sandra came back in with a long-sleeve shirt. Its surface had a waffled pattern like long johns. The shirt was old and dark blue; it reminded me of the type of shirt a construction worker would wear under his flannel.

"Thanks," I said. "For everything. I just need to rest for a while. In the morning I'll be gone."

"Eat whatever you want, I'll get you pants in the morning."

Steve and Sandra got up to go to bed. Steve slapped my back as he walked by and chuckled when I gasped. Sandra was only able to manage a weak smile as she passed me. The bedroom door closed quietly. I heard the wood rub against the jamb and then a loud slam completing the seal. I could hear the sound of quick discussion going on inside the room, but there was no yelling.

With my right hand I pulled the Glock from the holster at my back and put it on the table. Quietly I got up and moved to the fridge. There weren't any leftovers, so I took an apple. I winced as I bent to get it from the crisper. I ate the apple silently as I looked through the cupboards. I pulled a box of strawberry Pop-Tarts down and took them to the table. I ate the rest of the apple and the entire box of high-calorie pastries without pause. The sugary crap went down slow, but I was suddenly too exhausted to get up for a drink. When I was done, I slept face down at the table.

At seven-thirty Steve slapped my head lightly, waking me up. I put the Glock behind my back right away and looked at Steve.

"Pants," was all he said.

"Thirty-two in the waist and thirty-four in the leg. Some kind of work pants, khakis, the kind that won't rip easy."

I stood up, shakily, and gave Steve three twenties. "Grab some of those caffeine drinks too."

Steve left without another word, and I had three more apples. I sat with my legs crossed, waiting for Sandra to finish in the bathroom. She must have gone in while I was face down at the table. Twenty agonizing minutes later she walked past the kitchen, hair up in a towel, dressed in a faded pink robe. I moved slow into the foggy, cramped bathroom and sat, because, shaky as I was, it would be neater. When I finished, I looked in the mirror at the shirt Sandra had given me. It was clean; no blood had leaked through overnight. The pattern in the shirt even made the bulge of the bandage less noticeable.

Steve came back half an hour later as I was stretching in the kitchen, using one arm on the counter to stabilize me. The car crash, gunshot, and nap at the table had left me aching in every possible way. He threw the pants at me, and I managed to catch the bag with my right hand. I put it on the counter and pulled free the pants and two four packs of Red Bull. I put the holster and Glock on the counter and dropped my pants on the spot. If Steve cared he didn't show it. The work pants were olive green and they fit fine. Steve left the room as I transferred my belt to the new pants, and came back with a blue button-up oxford-cloth shirt.

"To cover up the gun," was all he said.

The shirt fit a little snug, but left unbuttoned it was a good fit, and it concealed the Glock better than the tight blue shirt.

I chugged three Red Bulls without pausing and smiled as the liquid caffeine hit me. "Steve," I said. "Thanks for everything."

"What are friends for? Car keys are in your pillowcase."

I yelled, "Thanks, Sandra."

She screamed something back about a doctor. As I picked up the pillowcase heavy with lockbox, laptops, and shotgun, I caught Steve's eye.

"You need me, you call," he said.

"I won't."

"You need me, you call," he said again, and then he turned around and walked back into the bedroom to see Sandra.

I went down the stairs riding an artificial buzz. I didn't slip and I didn't fall. My car was out back where Steve had said he left it. When I opened the door a heavy smell of cleaning products wafted off the interior. Steve must have given the car a once-over. I thought to myself, a friend who will clean up dried blood for you is a friend for life.

I drove back to the office without any swerving or accidents, parked the car, and slowly walked up the stairs to the office. I moved cautiously, but there was no one waiting for me in the stairs or the hallway.

In the office, I made a strong cup of tea and sat by the window, letting it work its magic. Outside the city had woken. People scurried out of their holes and went frantically to their posts. They all wore the same uniform at this hour. The men were in pleated pants, pressed shirts, ties, but no jackets. The women all had skirts of sensible lengths accessorized with sensible heels. These were the middle-class urban go-getters. They were into the office first, coffee in hand, and out last, migraine in head. They would all be promoted by thirty, and dead by fifty.

The minutes clicked by, and each second was marked by a throb in my arm. I went to the bathroom and brought back the bottle of Advil, using one arm and my teeth to force open the child-proof top. Eight of the pills went into my mouth, and I winced at the bitter taste underneath the sweet coating. I couldn't risk trying to get anything stronger from the contacts I had in the city. It would be a dead giveaway to anyone looking for a person who was shot last night. The hard stuff wouldn't help me now anyway. I had to keep my head clear for everything that was to come.

I winced as I got up and went to the closet. I clumsily moved the invisible panel out of the back of the closet with my one good arm. I put the shotgun in, knowing that I needed to get rid of it as soon as possible, and pulled out the cell phone I took off Igor. Getting the panel back in place was a challenge, but I managed — dampening my forehead with exertion in the process. I powered up the cell phone, dialled the number I had watched Mikhail enter not long ago. After two rings, I was greeted in Russian.

"Get me Sergei."

"I am very sorry," said a voice that suddenly contained no trace of an accent. "There is no one here by that name at this number."

"Tell him it's Wilson and it's done."

"I believe you are confused, sir. I think . . ."

"Do you have call display?"

"Sir, you are . . ."

"Do you have call display?"

"Yes sir, we do, but I don't . . ."

"Listen, you tell Sergei I'll be waiting for his call at this number."

I hung up the phone without another word and waited. It was one minute before Igor's cell phone chirped. I let it ring three times before I answered.

"*Da?*" I said.

There was a long pause before I heard a response. "You have what we spoke of?" It was the same calm, cool, heavily accented voice I'd heard before. The pause before he spoke let me know I had cracked the facade he was putting on.

"*Da,*" I said.

"Cut the shit. You are on thin ice as it is. You have done things no one would dare, and now you speak to me with a smart mouth?" The crack in his facade had burst wide open.

I thought of the death squad who attacked the computer geeks and decided to can the humour. "I have all of it."

"You are sure?"

"The disks and everything that touched them are here."

"You will bring it to the place you visited yesterday."

He didn't want to mention specifics, and that suited me fine, but in the shape I was in there was no way I could walk away from a meet with the Russians again. "No deal, Sergei. You will come pick it up at the same spot you sent those two shitheads to the other day."

"I told you to watch your mouth. You are testing my patience, boy."

"There's no way I'm walking into your house holding a bag that protects me right until I hand it over. You meet me. Come and claim your property, and I mean it like I said it. You claim it."

153

His voice got louder in the earpiece, and some of the *w*'s started to slip to *v*'s. "I will not come, I will send some associates of mine to collect my property. One of them remembers you, and demands to meet you again."

"When?"

"Soon. Stay put."

There wasn't much else I could do in the position I was in. I was hurt and outnumbered. I didn't have the time or the energy to scout out a spot for an exchange with Sergei's men. The office was the best spot I had. Sergei knew that I made it through an ambush here, and now I had the advantage of being here first — it was the only advantage I would have. He would have to be careful, and whoever he sent would have to be better than Igor and Gregor — much better. I couldn't fight it out with Sergei's men in the condition I was in. I needed insurance, so I got up and went to the pillowcase. I reached inside past the laptops, and thumbed open the latch on the lockbox. Inside was a stack of disks. The CDs were unlabelled and encrypted, so I had no idea which ones contained the most incriminating data. I pulled a disk from the middle of the stack and walked to my desk.

I was already fucked with the Italians. The poor Russian accent I used with the Voice would put Paolo off my scent, but he would suspect me eventually. I had time with Paolo. He wouldn't let on his suspicions to his crew because it would be an admission that he didn't trust them to run the job on the Russians. That kind of admission of doubt would hurt him. He would have to take me quietly with someone he trusted. Maybe Julian, once he healed. Whatever was coming from Paolo would take time, and time was something I didn't have with the Russians. Once I gave up what they wanted, I would be on the wrong side of a bullet. I stole from them and killed men from their

MIKE **KNOWLES**

ranks. I had to rely on the idea that whatever was on those disks was important enough to keep me breathing. A kill squad hit the blackmailing accountants with no mercy; that kind of brazen effort meant whatever was taken was worth more than the cost of the heat the police would bring. Even more telling was the urgency from the both sides. Everyone wanted me to finish the job quick. Paolo gave me a day before they would handle me themselves, and the Russians did the same. The short time frame from both sides meant one thing — war was coming. Taking the disks was an all-out declaration of war. But Paolo knew that the risk could be minimized if he could put the Russians off his scent and on to mine for a few days. That was all the time Paolo needed to decode the disks and turn them over to the cops or the media. The disks would decimate the Russian war party before it was mobilized. The Russians weren't going to let a coup like that go unchallenged, but they were without focus. They were working fast to get their property back, but the trail went cold with me. I didn't die as easy as the computer nerds. They couldn't force me to give up who I worked for so they had to settle for getting their property back; once they had it, they would find a way to make me talk. The disks were trouble from all sides, but holding on to one was the only way to keep me breathing.

I put the disk in an envelope and went searching, one-handed, for duct tape. The tape was with a number of other tools in the closet. I used the thick grey tape, tearing it with my teeth, to tape the envelope outside the window on the underside of the sill. The envelope matched the white concrete enough that it would be invisible from the street, and if the room was turned over fast it wouldn't be noticed unless someone held their head out the window. My life was taped outside the window, hanging in the breeze.

Once the disk was hidden, I got ready to meet the Russians. I didn't think they would be long. The information I had was important, and twice stolen; they would want to get their hands on it fast. I put the Glock on the desk, then got the SIG from the closet. I took the spare gun out of the oily rag it was wrapped in, and put it in the holster at my back. It took three tries to get the gun behind my back, but I could pull it free from the holster without a lot of trouble. I was slow in my condition, so the idea of pulling a spare gun was better than trying to reload. I stopped worrying about the gun and went to the washroom to relieve the urge from the Red Bulls and the tea. On the way back from the bathroom I put the kettle on again. The tea would take my mind off how tired, sore, and battered I was.

I waited in my chair, Glock in hand, drinking tea, for forty-seven minutes. It was then that the frosted glass of my door darkened as though an eclipse had occurred in the hall. The eclipse was the man I had shot at 22 Hess.

Ivan came in with another man who was much shorter than his towering height. They both had on dark jackets, pants, and shoes. The dark jackets were open, and their hands were empty. I had shot Ivan hoping to put him in his place. Shooting him had done nothing but terrify me. His lizard brain was operating as soon as he was hit.

I stared at Ivan, watching the abyss behind his eyes stare back at me. The crocodile eyes looked and me with a carnivorous interest, but the rest of him stayed impassive. I moved my gaze slowly to the smaller of the two men and saw that he was taking in the room systematically, left to right, floor to ceiling. Once he finished, his eyes rested on me.

I had my useless left arm resting on the desk. Underneath I held the Glock, safety off, in my lap. My palm was sweating against the grip, but there was no way I was going to wipe it off. I just gripped harder.

"Morning," I said. I got no response at all. "The stuff is behind you in the pillowcase."

The little one looked behind him at the pillowcase, and I understood the situation. The little one was the help; he looked at the bag because he was the one who was going to carry it. Ivan never looked. The stuff didn't interest him — I did. Ivan was here to kill me.

I made my play right away. "The bag has most of the data your boss wanted back."

The short one looked at me, blinked, looked again at the bag, and then to me once more. I brought the pistol up easy. The little one took a step back and moved his arm to his jacket.

"Put your hand down," I said with no menace in my voice. "I gave your boss back most of the stuff. Some I kept as insurance, a gesture of good faith. I gave some of the disks to . . . a friend, a friend I see every day. The disks I took are in an envelope addressed to a cop I know not to be dirty. If any of this deal comes back to bite me in the ass the disks will be passed on, and that clean cop will earn a huge medal taking down your whole organization."

"That wasn't what you were told to do!" The smaller Russian sounded petulant.

"I don't take direction well. I went as far as I was prepared to. Now I'm done. We're done."

"You were told what it would take to be done. This is not it." The little one was still petulant.

"This is how it works," I said. "There are no set rules in our game."

Ivan moved for the first time. He surprised me by turning away and picking up the bag. It wasn't his job to carry anything; the bag was a message. Ivan lifted the bag with the arm I shot, and opened the door with the other. The smaller man turned and left without being told. Ivan was the true heavy, the one in charge. He turned to me before leaving. "No rules in game," he said, and chuckled. His laugh was terrible. It was in the back of his throat, and it had the destructive sound of waves crashing on rocks. "Soon we be only game in town."

He left without closing the door behind him. I waited for ten minutes with my gun pointed at the open door. When my forearm started to ache, I got up and shut the door. I stumbled to the desk using any object I could to stay upright, and passed out at my desk face down with my gun still in my hand. My face had the idiot's grin of a survivor.

# CHAPTER TWELVE

I woke several hours later. The angle of the sun through the window told me it was midday, and the clock confirmed it. My mouth was dry, but my body was clammy. The bullet wound had given me a fever, and I had sweated through my shirt. I got up from the desk and tried to stretch. My bad arm barely made it ten inches from my body. I scrounged for another energy drink, finally finding one in the pile of things I brought with me from Steve's. I popped the top and ignored the spray of warm liquid that went all over my hand. The drink was too sweet, and it had almost a medicinal taste as it went down my throat. When the can was empty I rubbed my hands over my face, feeling the stubble, as I staggered to the window. I used my reflection to confirm my suspicions. I looked like hammered shit.

"Damn," was all I said to myself.

There was no question, I had one priority now. I had to get the bullet out of my arm, and I had to do it quietly. I had to avoid any off-the-books doctors that had any relation to anyone I knew. That meant I had to avoid doctors who dealt with people. I knew a veterinarian. She worked on horses out in the country. She was also a drunk. For enough cash to keep her drowning she would work on almost anyone. I came across her while I was chasing Donny O'Donnell, an Irish gangster and local psycho who had been raping women in Corktown for years. Corktown was in the southeast part of downtown; it was a historic Irish neighbourhood, and much of the Irish blood had never drained out. The whole neighbourhood was terrified of O'Donnell and his crew, so he went unchecked, growing more brazen with each attack. For his last attack, he happened to choose a woman who lived about a block outside his neighbourhood, and who had been a waitress for a catering company owned indirectly by Paolo Donati. Word of the assault got back to him, and with it came tales of the nightmare of the small Irish neighbourhood. I was given the task of bringing the neighbourhood terror to Paolo. I worked my way through O'Donnell's small world and came, first-hand, into contact with his legacy. I met men and women whose lives had been obliterated by a big sick fish in a small pond. I finally managed to catch up with him and put a bullet in his gut, but he vanished on me. There was no trace of him in the city. The horror stories I learned searching for the bastard kept me on his trail. After a few days, I found out that he was convalescing in the country. Exactly where was hard to find; I only knew he was with a vet out in the boonies. At first, I thought he was hiding with a war buddy, but he was too young to have been in any conflict that I could recall. O'Donnell was never a soldier; he was too much of an animal. That was when it hit me — animals go to a vet all their own. After a day of grinding through the crew O'Donnell left behind, I was pointed in the right direction — Flamboro.

I went out to Flamboro Downs racetrack and planted myself there for a few days. I played the part of a degenerate gambler looking for inside information. I asked about the animals' health, diet, and where they were tended to. Each day I checked out vets and names I overheard, and the next day I was back asking more questions. I finally caught a break when an old horse broke its front legs a mile out of eighth place.

"That one is off to Maggie's," I heard a man say.

I found out that the owner was broke, and Maggie was a disgraced, unlicensed vet who fixed horses passably or put them down cheap. A little more digging got me an address and a life story the locals seemed to revel in. Maggie lost a kid, then a husband, hit the bottle, and then lost everything else, including her licence.

I found her place that night, and her Irish patient left with me, without a word, while she was sleeping. I made sure he stayed in good health — for a while. Now, years later, with the Irish gang gone, she was the only doctor I knew who was completely off the grid to the people I was involved with.

I kept money in a few different places around the city. Some of it in banks — more in safe spots where people would never think to look for it. It wasn't the most secure idea, but it was accessible at all times. Now was one of those times. I would pull what I needed for the vet on my way out of the city. I moved to the closet and used my good arm to free a bag and a change of clothes. I put the clothes in the bag along with some food for the drive. I didn't put in any identification or items that would give me a name. I wanted to be in and out, fast and anonymous. Packing brought with it a bit of dizziness, so I sat at my desk and waited for it to pass. I passed out again face down at the desk.

The sound of the door splintering off its hinges brought me awake. The frosted pane cracked and the door swung open, slamming against the wall. The door ricocheted back slower, one corner dragging on the floor. I was startled straight up from my sleep. I reached my closest arm towards the Glock still on the desk, forgetting that it was useless. The shooting pain my stupidity caused cost me seconds I needed. I moved my right arm and got my hand on the gun just as I heard, "Don't do it, Wilson."

The two men in front of me were middle-aged Italians. They had short dark hair, crooked noses, and scar tissue around their eyes. They were not handsome men. Their misaligned features were augmented with layers of fat that hung on cheeks studded with blackheads. They were brothers of the same ugly mother.

"Hand off the gun. Get up now."

I didn't move. I was still groggy and a bit out of it. My brain was telling me something I couldn't process. I blinked hard, and the speaker, the ugly guy on the left holding a snub-nosed revolver, spoke again.

"Hand off the gun. Get up now."

My brain snapped into focus. These were the Scazzaro brothers — Johnny and Pat. They were mid-level muscle, and they were probably here because Julian couldn't be. I looked at Johnny and played through my mind everything he had told me. While I was thinking, he again told me to get up. He never said he would kill me, and he didn't even threaten to hurt me. He wanted me up so I could go somewhere.

"I know you're supposed to take me somewhere, not shoot me, Johnny. Put the gun down."

He didn't move. The gun wasn't pointed at me directly, but that could change quickly. I shifted in my seat, moving my body forward so the 9 mm still holstered at my back

MIKE KNOWLES

was away from the chair. I put a little agitation into my voice: "I'm serious. It makes me nervous when you point those things at me. What are you afraid of? I don't even have my gun in my hand, you caught me sleeping. If you're not going to kill me, and I'm not armed, at least point the gun at the floor."

The two brothers exchanged looks, but their guns never moved. I pushed harder. "If you're so fucking scared I'll give you my piece. Here!" With one motion I used my good arm and both feet to shove the desk over. The Glock hit the floor along with the overturned desk. Both men looked at the gun on the floor; they never noticed my hand moving behind my back, or it coming back with a pistol. When their eyes left the floor and found mine, it took five seconds for them to read my grin and move their eyes down from it to the gun in my right hand. The room didn't fill with noise, and bullets didn't rip me apart.

My gun was pointed at Johnny. He was the talker, so I put him down as the one in charge. "Where am I supposed to be going?"

The two exchanged glances out of their peripheral vision, unsure of the direction the discussion had taken.

"Boss wants to see you now," Johnny said.

"But he doesn't want me dead."

Johnny waited a second then spoke. "He said you crossed a line and he wanted your ass in front of him."

"Why send you two? Why not Julian?"

Pat sneered. "You know why," he said.

"No, I don't. Tell me," I said.

"Somebody hit Julian with a car. He says it was you. Boss wants to know what you got to say."

"You two are up to date on your gossip," I said. "Here's how we'll do this. You two are going to leave, and I'll go to the restaurant on my own."

"No. You're gonna come with us now. Like the boss said." Johnny's whiny voice let me know that he didn't like the sound of my idea. The gun in my hand meant things weren't going to go the way he planned.

"I'm going myself. Two shit button men aren't taking me anywhere. You want to see if you can make it otherwise, go ahead." The silence that followed told me they didn't. "I'll be along shortly, now fuck off."

Pat looked at Johnny for ten seconds, the two of them having a fraternal argument inside their heads. They both knew they were supposed to bring me in, not kill me, and the two of them weren't high enough on the food chain to make any executive decisions. They moved to the door, covering each other.

"We'll be waiting to follow you over, so don't get any ideas," was the only goodbye I got.

After they left, I ate everything I could hold down. I drank a Red Bull with a handful of Tylenol, changing it up from Advil. I picked up the Glock from the floor beside the desk and tucked it into the front of my pants with my right arm, making sure I could draw it without wincing. Once I got it right, I practised walking across the floor. I tried to hide any awkward movement, but I moved like I was in a jacket that was too small. It wasn't ideal, but it was the best I could do. Before walking out the door I rummaged in the garbage for an old newspaper. I knelt and used the floor and my one good arm to crease the paper in half. I nestled the SIG I showed to the Scazzaro brothers into the paper, folded it, and put it under my left arm.

The broken office door closed when I left, but it didn't hold. I left it as it was — I didn't have time to worry about it. Johnny and Pat weren't waiting for me in the hall or in the stairwell. No one was waiting outside, either, but a minute after I pulled the Volvo away from the building I picked up an obvious tail. The two Scazzaro brothers were behind me in a black SUV. Their worked-over faces appeared closer than they really were in the side mirrors. Pat was in the passenger seat talking on a cell phone. They weren't taking any chances getting me back. They would guide me in, and any hiccups would bring backup — quick. Traffic was light, and I only hit a few red lights. At each one I caught sight of a second black SUV farther back. I thought it was the person on the other end of Pat's cell phone — I found out later I was wrong.

As I drove, I glanced at the newspaper hiding the gun. It was an offensive, stupid idea, but it was necessary. A gun in plain sight should get me in the restaurant without frisking, provided I used the right attitude. I double-parked beside the cars lined outside the doors. The four guards out front weren't talking about sports, food, or women this time. They were looking at me like wolves eyeing a lone fawn.

I put the newspaper on my lap and took five deep breaths before I reached across my body and opened the door. I stood and tucked the paper under my bad arm, feeling the reassuring weight of the gun. There was no pain as long as I kept my left hand in my pocket.

"Move the car."

I ignored the order and started around the front bumper of the car.

"Hey, asshole, we ain't valets. Move the car."

As I passed the final corner of the bumper my right hand moved inside the paper under my left arm. The dampness of my fingers caused a small bit of friction on the newsprint. The four guards tensed when they saw my hand move. Each man's right arm moved a second behind mine.

"Easy, boys," I said as I approached. "I have some

business here today." I stopped in front of the group. "You know this place is watched, so keep your hands loose. If we start a gunfight no one leaves happy. I was told to come down and I'm here — on my terms. I'm going in, and you're staying here. Everyone watching this place will see me go in and everyone will see you stay out front as usual. You come inside and everyone watching will turn into everyone listening. When there ends up being something to hear, everyone will come in for a closer look."

I hoped my lies would play on the constant paranoia people in organized crime find themselves in every day. The men out front glorified themselves in their own minds. In their heads they were important, dangerous men. They could not imagine a group of law-enforcement officials who would not fear them, and therefore would want to keep constant tabs on them. In reality no one watched the restaurant all the time. If anything it was bugged by recorders that were collected and transcribed later. The law wouldn't know I came for months, if at all. Who knew if the tapes were even checked.

Four hard faces looked at me. Four hard faces saying nothing. I didn't wait for a response; instead I moved to the left of the group. If they drew guns they would have to move them across their bodies to get to me. The extra milliseconds would be necessary if I had to draw on them from under my arm. No one moved as I walked a semicircle around the group. I went through the door of the restaurant sideways, my eyes never leaving the small crowd of men. Once I was inside, I turned, and the newspaper followed my gaze towards the coat-check stall. Cold eyes greeted me, and one manicured hand was already under the counter.

"We've been here before."

The coat-check girl said nothing.

"And you know what? I'll still be through the door before you draw."

"I'm faster than I was," she said, her hand still under the counter.

I looked at her and let the grin form on my face. For a second her lips separated and her eyes found my hand in the newspaper pointed at her. She was instantly unsure of herself.

"It's good that you've gotten better. Me, I've never slowed down."

Her hand stayed under the counter as I went through the second set of doors.

I walked down the steps into the restaurant. All of the tables had chairs up on them as usual. The only difference was in the hallway where the booths were located. Two men stood there with guns in their hands.

# CHAPTER THIRTEEN

Neither of the two gunmen spoke to me. They took turns looking at me and at my hand in the newspaper under my arm. I took deep breaths and visualized shooting the one on the right and diving left toward the tables. I had to quickly re-evaluate my decision when I realized that my left arm couldn't take a bump on the floor; I'd have to shoot left and dive right.

"What in the hell did you do, *figlio?*" I heard Paolo before I saw him. He came out, empty-handed, from between the two men.

"The boys you sent didn't seem friendly. I decided I would come and see you myself. I meant no offence."

He stopped dead. "Don't you fucking lie to *me*, you stupid fuck. You took from *me* and attacked my people. You . . . you . . . fucked with *me*." Every *me* was emphasized like a sonic boom. Paolo was physically shaking. His rage dilated his pupils and made his hands shake. It turned him into the focal point of the room. No one could look anywhere else. "Then you lie to me like I'm worth nothing.

Not even an explanation. I bailed you out when you should have been dead. I gave you work when I should have made an example of you, and to reward my generosity you become Judas? What did it take to turn you, Judas? How much money, *figlio?*" Paolo's voice had worn down into a whisper; he was now the grand inquisitor.

I said nothing. The man calling me *son* wasn't my father; he kept me employed because it helped him. He hung me out to dry days ago for the same reason. I didn't argue back. I forced myself to stop hearing Paolo so I could focus. At some point I would be told to drop the newspaper. In my mind, I visualized tossing it in front of me and using the movement of the paper and the heavy sound of the gun hitting the ground to conceal my drawing of the other gun from my waistband. I watched myself in my head, over and over again, until I realized Paolo was staring at me.

"Thirty pieces of silver, eh Judas? You have no loyalty. I knew that when you first bit the hand that fed you. When a dog does that they put him down because they know that he's got a wild streak in him that's no good for nothin'. I made a mistake there. I thought you were better than a dog. But you're not better than a dog, you're still a crow. You come in here with a gun and lie to my face. To me! You cripple a man, my man, and then lie to me about it. Take off that shirt and we'll see the liar. Take it off! Show me you're not lying and I'll apologize for the invitation that offended you so much. I know what's under that shirt. I know because you didn't kill that kid, or his mom. That was always your problem. You only killed people you thought deserved it. You never saw that you were living in the jungle and everyone deserves it. The lions take who they want; they don't weigh out the morality of the situation — they just act. Acting is what makes them king

— not morality. I'm king of the fucking jungle. People die all the time because I say so, not because they deserve it — screw deserves. People die because I live. I'm what Darwin dreamed of at night. Top of the food chain, no remorse. Now take off your shirt."

"I did the job you wanted done. I picked up what you asked for. You lied. You never told me what I was dealing with."

"Risks, boy. Did you forget what you did for a living?"

"I never forget. I complete jobs that you need done. Jobs you want to be able to distance yourself from. I work for you, but I'm not your fall guy. You left me out to dry. You knew that the Russians would find me eventually. You knew they would have to work to find me and kill me, and you thought that in the time it would take them to do that you would be able to hurt them bad — maybe kill their organization completely. You set me up, and when that didn't work you sent men to bring me to you; to bring me to die. That's not how I work. My shirt stays on and I leave . . . for good."

"*Figlio.*" His voice was calm. "Do you know where you are? You don't show up at my place and tell me anything, and you don't quit — I fire you . . . for good."

Sensing the turn in the conversation, the two men raised their guns. The thug to my left said, "Put down the paper," in a cold, flat voice. I cursed myself for letting Paolo run the conversation and for getting me to talk. Since I had been shot I had just pushed forward, never stopping to plan. I was racing ahead while I was falling apart. My mouth let him get the better of me, and now I was at a disadvantage. Outgunned by two drawn pistols, I forced my knees to bend and my breathing to relax. I readied myself to shoot the man on the right. Two thumbs moved, and the guns in front of me cocked. The thug on the right repeated his order as the two men moved forward from the booths past Paolo, so that he was obscured from my view. We had fifteen feet between us.

I took one big breath and a step to the right table. "Okay, I'll put it down." My body started the turn, and I was about to let the paper fall when gunfire broke out.

I stopped and turned my head. Behind me, the sounds of gunfire popped again in the street. No one inside wasted time; four more bodies, armed with handguns, came out from the booths behind Paolo. The two men in front of me looked at Paolo for instructions; he had already decided what to do.

"Joey, go with them. Tony, watch Wilson."

Paolo went to the booths and picked up a revolver from a seat on the left. Tony, who stayed to watch me, had not moved his feet. He was looking to the door, back to me, then to Paolo.

"Get his shirt off," Paolo said. Tony looked at me, and I could see his eyes resist the urge to look anywhere else.

"Drop the paper," Tony said.

More gunfire sounded, closer now. It was automatic chatter, and it was replied to with single shots. I watched Paolo listen. Watched him realize he and his men were outgunned. Paolo and Tony looked over my shoulder toward the sound of approaching footsteps; I moved a few steps right, toward the kitchen.

"Boss!" Joey yelled as he rushed past me to Paolo's side as though he were a child afraid of thunder.

"What the fuck is going on out there?" Paolo roared as I took another few steps toward the kitchen. Paolo's eyes found me. "Tony, you make sure he stops moving."

"I'm putting the paper down. That's all," I said, and I slowly took the paper out from under my left arm to prove it to everyone.

"Boss, it's the Russians. They're in the street. They're killing everyone!"

Tony had his eyes on mine as I moved my arm to toss the paper toward the tabletop. We ignored Paolo and Joey's voices as they went over what was going on outside. I tossed the paper high and it landed with a loud thump. The sound interrupted the conversation and pulled everyone's eyes to the newspaper. No one watched my right arm move.

Three quick shots sounded; they were followed by a woman screaming, "No!" More automatic gunfire rang; its volume let us know it was just outside the dining room doors. Everyone's attention moved to the doors as I pulled my gun. I had it pointed at Tony for five seconds before he noticed it. His eyes moved to the barrel and grew wide. The only word he could find came out in a childish tone.

"Boss."

Paolo and Joey looked away from the door. Both saw the gun in my hand immediately.

"God damn it, Tony."

"Shut up, Paolo," I said. "The gunfire is slowing down, so we're going to have company soon. We need to get out of here. Is there a way out of here besides the front and the kitchen?"

"I don't run from no one. Especially those fucking commies."

"You can stay," I said. "But I want out, and if killing you gets me there I'll do it."

Tony and Joey brought their guns up. Yelling, "Boss, get down!" was all that stopped me from shooting them. The gunfire from Tony and Joey pushed three men back through the doorway, shattering the glass that led to the coat-check room. The men were clad in black, their pale white skin accentuated by the colour they wore. They took

173

cover from the gunfire in the coat-check area, but the darkness inside the room made it impossible to tell where.

No one moved. Muffled by the walls, a gunshot broke the silence; two more followed seconds later. There was a big gun outside.

I moved right, walking backward, keeping my eyes on the door, and on Joey, Tony, and Paolo, who had over-turned two tables for cover. When I got to the wall, I followed it to the far corner of the restaurant. I couldn't stay there exposed in the room for all to see. "Joey, Tony," I said. "I'm going to work my way behind you. The Russians are in a nasty choke point in there. They can't move out of it and into here without getting mowed down, even if you only have two guns. You start shooting at me, you'll lose focus, and the choke point. I'm moving behind you from your left."

"You stay put," one of them said.

"I'm not staying here. If this place is going to turn into the Alamo, it can do it without me."

I started moving down the wall toward Paolo, Joey, and Tony. To their credit Paolo's boys didn't look scared. They had a look of determination on their faces. Paolo just looked angry.

Joey and Tony kept their guns aimed at the door, but they stole looks at me out of the corners of their eyes. They were tense — waiting for an order to come. In a moment, I would be right behind them, and I knew they didn't want a gun behind them too.

I spoke to the two men, trying to sound as calm as possible. "Now, boys, I'm going to pass behind you. It would be smarter for you to keep your eyes on that door." As I spoke I noticed that my arm was getting tired from hold-ing the gun up. "Paolo," I said. "Tell them to let me by. You know it's a smart play."

174

After a pause Paolo spoke. "You two watch that door. If anything moves, you light it up."

"Thank you, Paolo," I said. Meaning it.

"Fuck you. We're not done. Not by a mile." The angrier he got the less philosophical he became; he spoke more like the thug he was destined to be, and less like the educated gangster he played at being.

I kept my gun trained on the door. I was a prime target alone on the wall without cover. I crouched low, trying to move knee to knee, but no one shot at me from the door. I didn't stop to wonder why it was so quiet behind the doors. I thought instead about the big gun outside. The front of the building was surrounded, and it wouldn't be long before the Russians tried to move through the doors into the dining room again. The Russians would kill me, and so would Paolo if he managed to get out of this alive. The back door was my only option. The fact that no one had come through the kitchen meant that the Russians were concentrating on the front door. They probably thought they could blitz through the restaurant like they did at 22 Hess, but Paolo's set-up was stronger than they expected. The Russians would regroup in the entryway, then hit the dining room hard. I had a small window of opportunity to get out alive.

"Paolo. What's out back?"

He didn't look over at me to answer; he kept his eyes on the door. "What do you think? You know the place. The alley is out back."

"I know about the alley," I said. "Tell me the layout. Everything you can remember."

"Why? You afraid you're gonna get lost running away?" He stopped then and considered his words and mine for a few seconds. "I heard those shots. You think someone's out front, huh?"

"Someone with a big gun. If I leave, I'll take him with me."

Paolo laughed at the idea and told me what I needed to know. "The door is heavy — all the doors here are. The locks are solid and expensive. Believe me. The door, it opens out."

"Describe the alley," I said. "The length and the width."

"It's brick on both sides; maybe ten feet wide. The whole alley is about a hundred feet long. There ain't a back way out — it's bricked off to the right. At the other end there's a side street that exits out to the main roads."

"That's not everything," I said. "Where does the trash go?"

"There's a Dumpster," Paolo said in a sort of "oh yeah" tone.

"Where is the Dumpster? Left or right?" I waited for the answer; it was fifty-fifty. Life or death.

"It's on the left."

The left, that one direction was my only hope. It was the fifty I wanted. I could work my way out of the alley using the Dumpster as cover. It wasn't ideal but it was better than the alternative.

I moved past Paolo's gunmen to the kitchen door. It was maroon, the colour of the walls, and it swung silently back and forth. Beside it was a row of five light switches set in a dingy brass plate. I eyed the coat-check room one last time before I moved through the door.

The kitchen was small and silver. The counters were clean, and the air was warm with dishwasher steam; the room was ready for the restaurant staff to start work in a few hours. The refrigerators hummed low, creating a background soundtrack.

The back door was just as it was described: heavy black metal with large, expensive locks. I took one final look around before I slowly started turning the deadbolts one after another. Each click got me closer and closer to outside. Each click brought more anticipation. On the final click, I stepped back from the door and took two deep breaths. I eased the door open a crack. Outside, in the crack of space that opened, I saw only darkness. I thought back and remembered the sun on my shoulders as I came in. I pushed the door open another two inches and still saw no light. The electric illumination of the kitchen lights revealed a dull, rust-speckled green outside the door. I tried to push the door open further but it wouldn't budge. It was the Dumpster; it had been moved right up to the door. I put the gun under the armpit of my bad arm and tried to shoulder the door open but the Dumpster wouldn't move. I gave up on the door and picked up my gun again. There was no one outside anymore. We were all locked in. It was then that I heard the shots.

There were three in all, and all of them came from a big, big gun. I remembered the echoed shots I had heard from outside and knew that everyone was inside the building now, and they were not going to stay in the coat-check area long.

I looked around the kitchen for another way out but I was stuck. There were no windows, and no other doors. I would have to go back the way I came. I moved to the swinging door. There had been no noise after the last three shots I heard. I doubted anyone could take Paolo, Tony, and Joey with three shots, but I had been wrong before.

The men in the coatroom had seen me cross the room. They knew where I was and they weren't going to let me live. I had to get out of the building, through Paolo and the Russians. I turned off all of the lights, making the kitchen black except for the light leaking in through the spaces in the door.

"Paolo," I yelled through the kitchen door. "Call for backup."

I could hear hushed mumbling, but nothing I could make sense of until someone yelled, "There he is, Tony. There, shoot him!" Three shots sounded, the first two close together, the last a second behind. One loud shot echoed back, and there was silence again. I waited three seconds then moved my arm out to the grimy light switch beside the kitchen door. I clicked every switch down with the flat of my palm. The room went dark instantaneously. The kitchen and the dining room were both black.

I slipped out the swinging door into the dining room. I kept low, stepped out beside the door using my shoulder to ease it quietly closed behind me. Once it was closed, I put my back against the wall just below the light switches. I couldn't turn them on again with my battered arm; it wouldn't extend anywhere near shoulder height, and if I used the other arm I wouldn't be able to shoot. I took a few breaths and began to slide my back up the wall. I felt the switches touch my back and I flattened closer to the wall. I waited for what felt like minutes until I heard the sound of footsteps on the stairs. One man can move silently, but more than one usually makes enough noise to be heard — especially in the dark. Five switches shifted up with a click under my back, and the lights immediately resumed their electric glow. Paolo was on the floor, shot in the stomach. The amount of blood told me that the bullet had not grazed him, but Paolo was alive with a gun in one hand and a cell phone in the other. Tony and Joey were dead. Their guns lay between them on the floor. At the top of the stairs stood Ivan and his huge gun. Behind him were three men dressed in black holding compact automatic weapons.

Ivan had his gun pointed down at Paolo's wounded

MIKE KNOWLES

body. His eyes and those of the men he was with were on me and the gun I was pointing at them.

"Feels like we've been here before, Ivan. You think you're going to do better the second time around?"

Ivan turned his head to me; his shoulders stayed square to Paolo. "We are here to win the game," he said.

"So this is checkmate. You take the king, and the board is yours?"

"The board belongs to us already. We are just making it permanent."

"The fuck you are, you commie bastards!" Paolo was alive on the floor, and he was making sure everyone knew it.

"Paolo," I said. "Did you make the call like I told you?"

"I'm gonna fucking piss on your graves, you motherless fucks."

"Paolo," I snapped. "Did you make the call?"

He didn't answer for a second that lasted minutes. "Yeah," he said. "I made the call. I couldn't say much, but I got the message across."

I couldn't be sure, because I wasn't looking in his direction, but it sounded like Paolo was smiling. "This looks like a stalemate, Ivan. There aren't any moves left. A new game is going to start soon."

Ivan said nothing to me. He spoke out to his men — in Russian.

"Don't do that," I said. "Keep it English."

Ivan didn't listen. He fired off more Russian in his thick, deep voice.

"Don't do that, Ivan." My voice was cold and serious.

Ivan stopped speaking, but it didn't sound abrupt. It sounded more like the end of a sentence — the end of a complete thought. He had issued a command to three men with guns, and I had no idea what he had said.

I couldn't read Ivan, so I focused on the three behind him, and the light switches against my back. One of the three was sweating heavily and looking at me out of the corner of his eye. He noticed my face and his eyes locked onto me as my mouth pulled tight into a grin. His eyes widened, and he looked to the other Russians. I dug my back into the light switches and shot the sweatiest gunman in the neck. Ivan's gun roared to life as I dragged my back across the switches. The room went dark for half a second, then Paolo fired his gun. The other two unnamed Russians returned fire at Paolo, then at the spot where I had been standing only seconds before. The bullets missed me, ripping into the wall at chest height. I was on the floor, sideways on my good shoulder, using the floor to steady my arm. The Russian henchmen were betrayed by their muzzle flashes. I saw their faces in the strobe light of automatic gunfire. I aimed at the man on the right and pulled the trigger. I quickly adjusted and shot left, where the second flashes had been moments before. I rolled forward from the wall toward the tables. I grunted as I hit my shoulder, but I kept moving. Automatic gunfire bit into the wall from across the room. I could only see under the tables so I had no idea where the shooter was. More shots rang out from my left. Paolo fired four bullets in quick succession, but their thunder was deafened by the metallic click of an empty gun that followed. The shots created two things in the darkness, a scream ahead of me, and a glimpse of a pair of shoes four feet in front of Paolo. I shot from the floor six times above where I had seen the shoes in the muzzle flash.

# CHAPTER FOURTEEN

The dark reeked of cordite, and my ears rang a far-off, high-pitched note. I managed to stand using the barrel of my gun to prop me up. I walked sideways until my crippled arm hit the wall. I hissed a sharp intake of breath, and then moved backward along the wall until I was massaged by five little plastic fingers. I used my shoulder to edge the switches up one by one. The first three lit up the rear of the restaurant; the final two lit above me and Paolo.

He was lying on the floor, leaking blood but still breathing. Ivan sat less than ten feet away. I had hit him in the shoulder and chest. The other four shots must have gone wild in the dark. In his hand, limp at his side, he still held his huge gun — another Colt Python. Paolo's eyes went wide when he saw Ivan sitting up with his gun still in his hand.

"Wilson, he's still got a gun. Wilson? Shoot him! Wilson, shoot!"

His screaming seemed to drive Ivan on. The Russian was working at raising his gun. It moved inches off the ground, then nosedived. It rose again, a few inches higher, using the bounce off the ground for momentum.

"Wilson." Paolo was pleading. *"Figlio,* please . . . shoot him."

Ivan's gun was four inches off the floor, and shaking as I moved toward Paolo. I had to laugh. "King of the jungle."

I looked at Ivan working so hard to get his gun six more inches into the air. I looked at him and said something I knew he would never understand. "You're dinosaurs, both of you. Too busy to notice the meteor."

Ivan might have been puzzled, but it was only for a second. The bullet made everything clear. Paolo grunted his appreciation and slumped to the floor. "Good job, *figlio*. Now pass me the phone."

I looked at Paolo and felt my finger hot on the trigger. I thought about killing him and ending my problems. But then I'd still have to deal with the Russians, and the rest of Paolo's crew once Julian told them I was finally open season.

"Are you and me even? For the disks, for Julian, for Tommy, for everything?"

Paolo eyed the gun in my hand and nodded. "Yes, yes, all is forgiven, *figlio*. Now give me the phone." The look in my eyes told him he would have to do better. "Fuck, after what happened today, I'm going to have more work than ever for you."

I looked around at the carnage in the restaurant. My eyes took in all of the bodies on the floor, and all the holes in the walls. I finally rested my gaze on Ivan, who was no less terrifying in death. His gun remained in his hand as though his body was still fighting even after it was left without a soul. I thought about how many times I had shot the huge man in the last few days and almost laughed. This was what Paolo offered. What his work would bring.

"I don't want more work. I know what you are, and I know what you think of me. I'm going to disappear. Don't look for me. Stay in your jungle and deal with the Russians."

I eased my finger off the trigger and walked away from Paolo. Behind me I heard a whimper from the top of the food chain, then a sob as he reached for his phone.